Love

&

Trap Houses:

Atlanta

By Sevyn McCray

Acknowledgments:

This is going to be short but sweet. To my children, Mahlik and Mahliya I thank you so much for giving me a break to do what I love. To all of my readers... I love each and every one of you. Thank you for buying my books, thank you for reading my books and thank you for telling others about my books. To my family and I mean this word "family" THE BANKROLL SQUAD, y'all rock. To the dolls in the Dollhouse, & G.I. Joe, 'Mama Peach' love u to death. My 'partna' in crime Chanel thanks for being the Robin to my Batman. We make this shish work. And to my girls/sistas.... You chics rock!!!!!

I dedicate this book to my brothers.... My lucky 7's. You are with me always Dino (Big Puncho) and Randy (R.J.) To my Stepfather James E. McCray, R.I.P. The first man to show me what a REAL MAN is. Thank you for being my Angel and my Superman.

Prologue:

"Max, Max, Maxxxxxxxx!!!!" she screamed up the back steps in their gourmet kitchen toward the master suite. When she didn't get an answer, she started to scramble the eggs the way she knew he liked them.

This would be the last meal that she would be cooking for her longtime fiancé. The next meal that she cooked him, she would be cooking for him as his wife. She was so excited. They were getting married at the Georgia Aquarium this weekend and what started out as a small intimate wedding had turned into a gathering of the who is who of Atlanta. Last time she checked, they had already spent two hundred thousand dollars on the wedding and she still had to close out her tab with some of the contractors.

Max had to go away on business and he wouldn't be coming back until late Friday evening. He tip toed up on the love of his life and wrapped his arms around her waist. "It smells heavenly in here my beautiful Blue. You know I love it when you are in the kitchen and barefoot. I just need you pregnant and the picture would be perfect."

Azure turned around and faced Max trying to hide her emotions. She had tested positive three days ago and was waiting to tell him about her pregnancy. "Aren't you the caveman, Maximillion? Barefoot, pregnant, and in the kitchen, I bet that would turn you on wouldn't it?

"Would it? You just don't know, just the thought gives me an instant hard on." He looked into her deep blue eyes and grabbed her hand and placed it on his penis that was bulging in his Ralph Lauren boxer briefs.

"Whoa there, calm down cowboy. Do you want me to finish cooking you breakfast or do you want sex on the counter?" Azure asked him as she broke from his embrace.

"I'm the king in this castle, I want both." Maximillion smiled showing his mouth full of braces.

"I swear your parents named you the wrong name, you take that emperor shit to a whole different level," she said as she put fresh fruit on the plate with the perfect scrambled eggs, French toast, and turkey bacon.

Max grabbed the plate, smacked her on her almost naked butt, and headed over to the island to sit down and eat. He sat down and dug in immediately. "Babe, you got enough money to clear the rest of the tabs? I want everything clear before my plane takes off this evening. All I want to have to worry about now is showing up."

"I got some money that I need to pick up this morning, that should be enough. If not I can go to the bank. " Azure stomach had been queasy the last past week, that was what made her take the pregnancy test. She sipped on her orange juice slowly.

"You still working? When are you going to stop? Come on now Blue, I told you months ago, that I had this. You are supposed to be working on the plans for your boutique, but you still pushing numbers. Damnit! What do I have to do for you to stop? You got six digits in your personal bank account. Then we have two joint accounts, overseas accounts, and you still working. I just want you to know that it's an insult. I can and will provide for you. You might as well still be in the club stripping." Outrage filled Max's voice. His fiancé was addicted to money and he could only blame it on the fact that she grew up so poor.

"I wanted this, this is my dream wedding. You would've been satisfied if we went downtown to the Fulton County Courthouse. I'm not the traditional girl; I don't have a father to pay for it. I was not about to let you spend all your money on this wedding." Even if her stomach wasn't queasy, this conversation would've killed her appetite.

"I try to stand my ground as firm as possible without being a bully, but this shit has to end. When I get back Friday, I want all the cards, card readers, printers, computers, and paperwork out of here. That will be your home office for the boutique. You have been training your cousin to take over. Both of us can't be in the streets. You have enough, what is mines will really be yours."

"Barefoot, pregnant, and in the kitchen. Tuhh," Azure scoffed at Max across the island as she felt the orange juice getting ready to come up.

"You forgot to mention felony free and beautiful business owner of a successful boutique. Time to cut the bullshit out and I mean it. Enough is enough and this is the last time we are having this conversation." Max got up and put his empty plate in the sink and turned to head up the back steps when he heard the first boom.

Chapter 1:

She hadn't slept in two days. Her time was getting near. Azure lie with her hands under her head and looked at the calendar that she had made with crayons that hung on the wall opposite her bunk.

There were only two more blank spots before her wake up. She had a plan to put into effect as soon as she set her feet on the pavement and she wasn't going to let up until she achieved her goal.

She was going to walk out the gate of the Tallahassee Federal Correctional Institute a new person. That is all that she could be. Her entire life had changed and what she had been through was either going to make her bitter or better. The letters from Max had stopped in her first year.

Not receiving any correspondence from him didn't stop her love for him. She still loved him just as much as she loved him the last time she'd seen him.

It wasn't her fault that they were locked up, but she had to admit that she played a big role in how much time they got. She felt guilty every day when she thought about the fact that Max took the bank fraud charge for her. He had nothing to do with her business. He had been trying to get her to stop her white-collar crimes for the longest.

He hated the day she ever got her hands dirty with the Nigerians, who turned her on to this money scheme.

The feds came to their house looking for guns, drugs, and money, but they found a whole lot more. All of her tools of the trade and cash on hand landed them with a bank fraud charge, along with the conspiracy, drug trafficking, and weapons charges.

Before she could even take responsibility for the automatic federal charges of bank fraud, the public defender notified her that her fiancé had taken all of the charges.

Shocked beyond belief, Azure wrote a letter to Max and sent it home to her cousin Fatt Mama, who was really a girl from the neighborhood who Aunt Nellie raised, as well. All she had to do was send the letter to Max because correspondence between two inmates at any federal prison was prohibited.

A few days later, she received a thank you card and on the inside it simply said, "I promised I would always take care of you. You should have just had enough faith to believe in me."

Heartbroken because she took those words to mean that if she had just trusted him, they wouldn't be as messed up as they were. She sent him a thank you card back the following day via Fatt Mama that said, "You are going to be a father."

She didn't receive another letter from Max for another two years and it was through one of his underbosses, Rocky. He was always brief. This time it was a sympathy card. The inside simply said, "You left me for dead, and they left you for dead. Blood don't make you family, Loyalty do. If you don't have blood and you don't have loyalty, that bitch ain't your family."

Now three years later, all of it made sense and Azure was ready to start where she left off at, but the key piece was missing, Maximillion Stevens, the only man to ever love her. She wouldn't be content until her king was free and back on the throne.

Chapter 2:

The fourteen-foot metal fence topped with razor, sharp, barbed wire slowly closed as if she was going to change her mind and run back inside. Today, August 16, 2013 was the first day of the rest of her life.

All of her belongings were inside two brown paper bags. Azure turned and looked back at the Tallahassee Federal Correctional Institute one last time before she mounted the steps to get on the Greyhound bus headed to Atlanta.

She made sure the only person that knew she was coming home was Aunt Nellie. She had long since cut off all ties with Fatt Mama. Her bunk mate, Bebe, had told her that she should've went fed on Fatt Mama and got her time reduced. She couldn't though; she just wasn't built like that. Azure wanted to make sure she was witness to Fatt Mama's demise. She was definitely on her list of things to do. She was going to get hers.

Now that she was free and her feet had touched the pavement as a free person, her adrenaline was dying down and her eyes were getting low as she put the two bags under her seat and settled in.

By the time the bus moved through the city and made it to the highway, Azure was fast asleep. When she woke up she wanted to be looking at the skyline of her hometown, Atlanta.

Even though she had gone through pure living hell while in prison those five years, she never had nightmares. Whenever she closed her eyes to sleep, she only thought about the greatest time of her life. Times with her and Max, they were always inseparable. They were the true definition of Bonnie and Clyde.

****

"Baby, pass me that small Pyrex pot from that cabinet over there." Max's chocolate baldhead shined under the kitchen lights as he moved around with an unlit blunt hanging from his lips.

Azure reached and got the pot and carried it over to where he was standing. His skin looked like milk chocolate against the stark white of the wife beater that he had on. "I guess this is my queue to leave," she said as she grabbed the blunt from his lips and reached into the pockets of her tight fitting Seven jeans and got a lighter.

She lit the blunt and pulled on it really hard inhaling the smoke into her lungs. She held it in too long and she started choking and coughing loudly, as tears rolled down her cheeks.

"My beautiful Blue, this is that grown man baby. You can't handle this like that shit you be over there smoking with your cousins." Max laughed at her as he walked up to her and wiped the tears from her face before kissing her on her button nose.

"Grown man hell, that is that grand daddy. Nigga my lungs burning. I don't want this shit, it feel like I'm on fire on the inside." She watched him as he pulled the blunt and blew out the smoke in perfect circles.

Max put the blunt out in the ashtray and got back to working. He could feel Azure's eyes boring into him as he moved around measuring the off white powder and Arm & Hammer baking soda in the beakers, adding the water, and stirring.

She didn't break her gaze and he didn't break his concentration. He usually would tell her to let him work. Not this time, she might as well learn the ends and out of the game. She had to know that it was more than just bagging it up and selling it to people.

After watching him for close to five minutes without him telling her to leave, she pulled up the bar stool, sat down, and studied him intently. She was amazed. She never knew that it required this much concentration and detail to mixing and making crack.

But she had heard long before she started dating Max that he was one of the best cooks on the Westside. This wasn't something any run of the mill nigga on the street could do; you had to be smart to perfect this. No wonder Max was so well respected.

He opened the freezer and got out the ice cubes and dropped them into the small, medium, and large Pyrex pots that he was cooling on the stove. Max had gotten so good with the cook game, the batches that used to take him all day to cook; he now cooked in less than an hour.

He still had to cut and bag up the soft coke for all his customers who still snorted it. He also liked to have a few ounces of pure already bagged up for his customers who cooked their own product.

Her eyes beamed with pride when he came over and motioned for her to kiss him on his lips. Standing only five feet two inches to his six foot three frame, she stood on her tiptoes as she kissed him softly on his lips.

His hands still had cocaine residue on it. He dusted the majority of it off on the front of his jeans before he put his hands in the back pockets of her jeans and palmed her round ass as he stuck his tongue in her mouth.

"That was amazing, I felt like I was in science class. Where did you learn to do that?" Azure asked Max as she wrapped her arms around his waist.

"Move in with me?" He wanted to change the subject, but he was even surprised when that came out his mouth.

Shock was written across her face, Azure's blue eyes darted back and forth looking around. "In here?"

"Hell nawl, my lady ain't fin to be living in no trap house," Max said with his brows furrowed looking at her seriously.

"Oh, so I'm your lady now, huh?" Azure said, jokingly as she tried to push him off her playfully.

He grabbed her tightly. "You were my lady the first week that we woke up in each other's face continuously morning after morning. Only a woman who loved me would put up with the way my breath smells first thing in the morning with all these damn teeth in my mouth."

Azure couldn't help but bust out laughing; she tried to control her laughter. She often looked at all the money he flashed around continuously, the jewelry, the clothes, and the fly rides and wondered why this man walked around with his mouth looking like that.

She knew he had at least six extra teeth in his mouth. No one could be perfect; at least he knew his grill was fucked up. Now that was what you called a gangster grill.

"Oh, really now! This is news to me. I guess I'm going to have to tell Trey Songz that I got a man now." Azure laughed really loudly.

"Out of all the men in the world, you would say Trey Songz. So, that is what you want, an ol' R & B nigga. You want somebody who is going throw his dick around and sang to you while he sweating. Girl if you don't get out of town. This is what you really want." Max pulled up his shirt and revealed a small round protruding belly.

"Yo azz need to do some sit ups, looking like you are at least two months pregnant and don't blame that on getting money either. This is not eating healthy." She rubbed his stomach in a circular motion.

Chapter 3:

"Auntie, Auntie, Auuuuuuuuuntie," Azure hollered as looked at all the old clothes on the bed.

"Why you calling me like that? This is not your mansion. This house ain't but so big. What is your problem chile?" Aunt Nellie walked slowly into Azure's bedroom. She was so happy that her niece was home from prison. Those five years seemed like twenty. She was the only family that she had left.

"I don't have anything to put on. What am I going to do? This is the first night that I decided to go out after being in this house a month. I have to go to this party," Azure whined, looking at her grandmother's sister, who had been there since the first day that she was born. She was the one who named her.

"You have went down at least five dress sizes while you were in prison. If I looked fine as you, shit I would just go to the club naked. I bet you could get all the men. Lord knows something needs to happen. You sitting around here waiting on Max to come to his senses, it's time to live your life. You have a new start on life; use it. Don't waste the rest of your life waiting on that man. Men come a dime a dozen," Aunt Nellie said, wanting Azure to get out of this slump that she had been in every since she came home from prison.

"Men like Maximillion Stevens are like a needle in a haystack. He is one in a million. I will never find another man like that. I need to be close to him. I just need to talk to him. Once I hear his voice, once I get a chance to tell him everything I know I will be better."

She gave up on wearing any of her old clothes as she plopped down on the bed on top of the massive mound. The majority of her things were outdated, but that was the one thing about couture or certain designers, it was timeless.

All her jeans were designer. She could throw on a V-neck or wife beater and a pair of her designer heels and grab one of her Louis bags and pull off the look. The big problem was, she could no longer wear the jeans.

"Girl fix your face." Aunt Nellie went into her bra and pulled out a bankroll and peeled off ten one hundred dollar bills.

"Don't tell me you been holding out on me little lady." Azure bounced off the bed and gave her aunt a hug before snatching the money out her hand.

"You took care of me good before you got locked up. I always been a saver and I always had more than one source of revenue. I got money put up. You made sure that this house got paid for. All I got is a light bill and car insurance. I still get the check from Benny being in the army and plus I get my Social Security and retirement." It made Aunt Nellie happy to see her niece smile.

"Let me find out…" Azure bounced out the room and grabbed the keys to her Mercedes truck.

"Get something done to that hair while you out. I'm tired of seeing it up in a ponytail. Call Fatt Mama and ask her who do her hair. It always looks so nice. You haven't seen her since you been home."

"Excuse my language for at least sixty seconds. Fuck that fat bitch. I wouldn't let a muthafucka that put they hands in her head wipe the shit out the crack of my ass. I don't fuck with her and let that be that. It's all gonna come out soon enough. Quit trying to force her on me. The only thing you doing is speeding up her demise. Let me continue to plot and plan. I'm good, the only people I need are you and Max."

"I will be happy when you finally tell me what that damn girl did to you. Every time she calls or come by I act like I'm busy so she hurry up and leave."

"Keep doing that, I don't want you in the middle of any of this. Remember that I am blood, though." Azure walked out the door and got into her truck as the

17

memories of when her and Maximillion went to the dealership to pick it out flooded her mind.

"You need to put this in your Aunt Nellie's name," he said as he whipped his pride and joy down Peachtree Road.

The 1969 Chevy Camaro SS commanded attention and it was in showroom condition. It never failed that they were approached constantly with offers to buy it from him.

"Why? Baby this will be my first time buying me a luxury car from a dealership. I want it to be in my name. This is going to be brand new. I will be the first owner. For me, this is a major accomplishment." Whining usually got Azure what she wanted.

"Aunt Nellie was on her job for her almost fifty years. She is a homeowner, and she is the widow of a war hero. She can afford to come in and give these people ten or fifteen thousand dollars at a time without batting an eye. You are only twenty-three years old and you don't have any property or businesses. Use your head beautiful Blue." Max pulled into the dealership.

She looked at him as her eyes watered. She had fifteen thousand dollars cash in her purse ready to put down on the truck that they had saw last week when they were on vacation in Miami.

That was all she had been talking about because nobody was riding them like that in Atlanta. She wanted the truck right now, but Max wanted her to wait. Azure wiped her eyes and looked over at him.

"There is no use in me going inside. I know what I want. I got the money for what I want, lets go and get Aunt Nellie."

As she thought about it, it was always Max with the level head. It was because of Max that she still had her truck and it was paid for with less than twenty five thousand miles on it. Tears started to pour down her face as she put the car in reverse and headed to Phipps plaza to get a pair of jeans. Her heart was in so much pain, without Max; she didn't want to exist.

Azure opened the sunroof and turned the music up. She still had satellite radio, Ashanti and Robin Thicke came on and before she knew it she had to get off at the Howell Mill road exit because she couldn't stop the tears from flowing. She proposed to Max while this song was playing in the background.

She valued her Aunt Nellie's opinion, but she had to go and get her man. That is all her mind was focused on and attending the big party tonight at Luxurious was definitely the first step.

Chapter 4:

She valet parked her truck and nervously walked to the front of the V.I.P. line. Butterflies filled her stomach as she rubbed her sweaty palms on the front of her R13 jeans and smiled at the people in the line. You couldn't tell from the aura that she gave off that she had been locked up or that she was broke.

Azure acted like royalty as she flashed her beautiful, Vaseline coated smile at security and turned to the hostess seated at the door with the clipboard in hand. "Azure Knight."

"Which party are you attending ma'am? We have three tonight," the young lady said, staring at Azure trying to see if those were her eyes or contact lenses.

"I'm here for Rocky's party." She tapped the toe of her Jimmy Choo wedge sandals as she waited for the hostess to look through the list for her name. She knew her name wasn't on the list, but hell it didn't hurt to try. She had made it this far; she planned on just pulling out a hundred dollar bill and passing it to her.

"You need to be coming to King's party beautiful," the voice filled with baritone behind her said. She wanted to start laughing because he sounded like James Earl Jones on 'Coming to America'. Azure had to turn around and see who the voice belonged to.

"She with me, miss lady." He linked his arm in hers and walked her through the front door of the club.

Azure blinked her eyes hard to adjust to the light change. She pulled away from the guy who had escorted her in the club. She was on a mission. She needed to find Rocky.

"Damn lil' mama, that is how you going to treat a nigga after he got you in the club. You obviously don't know who I am?" he said as he stuck his chest out proudly, smiling showing his top and bottom grill.

"Nawl, lil' buddy you must don't know who I am. I was going to get in this club with no problem without you. You just sped up the process. Money talks from dust to dawn. I preciate it you tho' parna." Azure left him standing in the middle of the floor looking at her back as she walked toward the biggest V. I. P. area.

He had to find out who she was. She had to be new in town, although she did look a little familiar. There was no way possible she didn't know who he was. His V.I.P. area was steadily filling up, but as he looked across the club Mustafa saw that Rocky's V.I.P. was spilling over with the who is who and the girl was right in the middle of it, in deep conversation with Rocky.

21

Azure rubbed her hands down the front of her jeans one last time and took a deep breath before taking the last steps toward the people who were the closest to her before her incarceration. She knew that she looked different. But it was two things that wouldn't change about her, her height and her eyes. It seemed like the closer she got to the group the louder her heartbeat in her ears. She no longer heard the music.

She didn't think that she stood out; she actually wanted to fade in with the crowd. She had on a pair of jeans, a wife beater that she had bought from the gas station, and a pair of six-year-old Jimmy Choo's.

She cut it up to where it only covered her breast. Her chiseled abs looked like sheer perfection. Her tight thighs and round ass made Azure a showstopper regardless of what she had on, but she carried her self like royalty.

"Your still beautiful Blue." Rocky recognized her when she walked in with King.

Azure turned around and jumped into Rocky's humongous arms. "Big brother, I have missed you so much."

"I can't tell," he said smugly as he placed her back on the floor. He could feel all the eyes on him. Her face seemed the same yet different. Her dyed jet-black hair was gone and replaced with what he took for her natural color, a copper with blonde streaks. It was no longer straight; it was naturally coiled around her face that was slimmer and lighter.

Never fat or even what he would call chubby, Azure was thick more than anything, but in all the right places. Now she was sculpted and chiseled. Her eyes were still blue, but they were empty and Rocky knew why. No Max!

"I had to come here to see you. I will do anything if you could just get Max to call me. I have to hear his voice. Please Rocky, do that for me!" Azure pleaded with him.

"Okay, what is your number? And what da hell you doing walking in here on the arm of King?" Rocky asked as he pulled out a phone that was almost big as his hand.

Azure screwed her face up. "King? Y'all call that clown King? Talk about instant ego booster." She looked in the direction that she walked from and seen that the man who escorted her in the door was now surrounded with dozens of people who all seemed to be vying for his attention.

"That is his name. Come on now aren't you the one to talk. Your name is Blue night." Rocky burst out laughing.

"Fool my name is Azure Knight. Big difference, big, huge difference. And that is Knight with a K.'" She missed the camaraderie that she had with all of Max's homeboys. It meant a lot to her especially since she was an only child.

Rocky reached out and touched the scar on her face, it was an ugly scar, but it some how managed to look beautiful on her. "We've missed you sis. Come say hello to everyone so that they can stop staring so hard."

"I'm not ready yet. There will be a time for everything." Even though her wedges were at least five inches, she still was a lot shorter than Rocky. Azure stood on her tiptoes and gave him a kiss on the cheek and a hug before allowing him to return to his party.

She walked a few steps before turning around; he was watching her smiling with glee. He held up the thumbs up sign then saluted her three times. That was one of the crew signals that Max had.

As she got closer to the door, she was literally swept off her feet as the man who escorted her in, picked her up off the ground. His intoxicating cologne combined with Kush assaulted her senses. But it was his beautiful childlike smile that sealed the deal.

"You can't be leaving? We haven't sung happy birthday yet," he said, looking into her eyes. He felt like he was drowning in them. Right away he knew who this was. This was Mad Max ol' lady. It had to be, but he thought that she got banged up with Max.

"Oh, it's your birthday sir? Well happy birthday. Hope you enjoy. Thanks again for allowing me to walk in with you, Blessing of many more outstanding birthdays. Have a good night." Azure pulled away from his grasp and started toward the door again. She really didn't want too many people to recognize her. Her mission was complete for tonight.

"Let me take you to brunch tomorrow. Here is my number. My name is King." He reached into the back pocket of his Purple Label slacks and pulled out a wallet. King put the business card in her open palm.

Without glancing at it, Azure placed the card in her army fatigued Louis Speedy bag. "Okay I will get in contact with you tomorrow. But one quick question... what is your real name cause there is only one man who I will ever call King?" Azure raised her eyebrow and folded her arms.

"Mustafa, King Mustafa," he said with a smirk still mesmerized by her eyes.

"Goodnight Mustafa." She walked away quickly, but she felt his eyes boring into her back.

Chapter 5:

She had been sick ever since she got to Tallahassee. She was literally starving. She couldn't stand the food. Azure couldn't understand why she didn't have any money on her account. Fatt Mama usually made sure that she was straight. She hadn't talked to her since she made it to the prison.

With one dollar left, she emailed Fatt Mama again from her CorrLinks email account and hoped she responded. Her stomach growled as she got up to go to the shower. Lil' Max was hungry.

Azure rubbed her stomach as she grabbed the thin towel and the small piece of soap that they gave her when she came in.

She didn't make any friends when she was at GEO and she wasn't trying to make no friends here. She had sixty months, but if Fatt Mama did like she said and sold some of her jewelry, she will be out even sooner. She needed a paid lawyer.

Max had wanted her to use his lawyer that he had on retainer. If he didn't do anything else faithfully, he made sure he paid his lawyer a thousand dollars a month to keep him on retainer. She wanted all the money that he

26

had socked away on his lawyer to go towards him since he was bearing the weight of all the charges. Her public defender wasn't so bad. It helped that she was a young girl from Atlanta, as well.

She had heard of it being no hot water, but never no cold water as the water scalded her. She closed her eyes and just dealt with it. This was the first time she bathed in the three days since she'd been here.

Maybe she needed the hot water to cleanse her. It was under the burning water that she let the realization finally set in. She was twenty-three years old, pregnant, and locked up in the federal penitentiary. Azure cried silently, the tears pouring for her unknown future, her unborn child, and for the fact that she was away from her better half Max.

The water was suddenly turned off and she felt something sharp pressing up against her back.

"I heard we just got a ripe Georgia peach in here so I decided to get the first taste. I love peaches, that is my favorite fruit," the husky voice said into the ear of the girl.

She sniffled one time and all kinds of thoughts went through her head. She'd never been the one to wear an ass whooping. The phlegm that had built up from when she was crying was salty tasting in her mouth. All she could think about was being violated while she was pregnant.

One of the best things about being small was being quick. Azure turned around with the speed of lightning and spit the hunk of phlegm in the face of an overweight, dark skinned girl.

She then knocked the shank out of her hand and took the palm of her hand to the girl's nose. Shocked, the girl instantly grabbed her nose with both hands as blood spilled everywhere and when she did that Azure kneed her in her stomach with brutal force again and again.

Azure didn't remember what happened next or getting jumped in the shower. She woke up in the prison's infirmary six days later with her head wrapped up, her jaw wired, and her body empty and in pain.

"Get up chile and help me put these roses somewhere. The entire living room and dining room is filled with them. Who in the hell did you meet when you went out last night? Prince Charming?" Aunt Nellie asked as she stood over Azure who seemed to be deep in sleep until she walked in on her.

Azure had never been so happy to hear her aunt's voice. She couldn't remember the last time she had a nightmare, she just prayed she didn't have anymore. To live through that once was enough. She stretched her body out in her queen size platform bed just to make sure she didn't feel any of the pain from five years ago. No physical pain, but the emotional pain would never disappear. Her hand instantly went to her flat mid-section.

"What roses honey? I don't smell roses, but I do smell your hot buttered biscuits. Azure jumped out the bed quickly, kissed her aunt's cheek, and rushed into her bathroom to brush her teeth.

When she walked into the living room, it was filled with vases of roses that covered every flat surface. Colors that she didn't even know that roses came in. The smell was so powerful that she no longer smelled the breakfast that Aunt Nellie was cooking. But that didn't stop her stomach from growling.

In the center of the dining room table was eggs scrambled just the way she liked them with extra cheese, bell peppers, mushrooms and onions, Creamy grits, biscuits and cut up melon. Surrounding the food was even more roses.

"Fix ya plate and tell me about Prince Charming," Aunt Nellie said as she sat down at the table.

Azure grabbed the small envelope out of the dozen of red roses before she sat down to join her aunt. She felt her gaze on her as she waited patiently for her to open the card. "Not Prince Charming Auntie, more like King Mustafa."

"The King Mustafa? You was with him last night? Ain't he fine chile? And that voice, remind me of Barry White, mixed with a little Teddy P'. That is Hattie Mae's grandson. I play bingo with her every week. I met him when I went to visit her in the hospital when she broke

29

her hip. That boy is rich. I mean richer that you and Max was. He got businesses. A lot of em'"

"Well Auntie, that boy wanna take yo' niece out to brunch today," Azure said as she stuffed her mouth with the delicious food. She knew she would have to go running as soon as she finished because her aunt was trying to get her back fat.

"Brunch, you don't got nothing to wear to brunch all yo' damn clothes too big." Aunt Nellie grabbed the empty plate from in front of her niece and placed it in the sink.

"Don't remind me. But I can always raid your closet. You got clothes for days and all you ever wear is your church suits and your house dresses. I know I can find something in there." Azure walked toward her aunt's bedroom. She remembered when she took her to Haverty's to refurnish her house with the best of the best. It was like she was foreshadowing the fact that someday it would become her home again.

Aunt Nellie was only one hundred pounds soaking wet and not even five inches tall. Azure knew she could find a dress and maybe put a belt on it or something to dress it up. She made her clothes, clothes never made her. She opened her aunt's closet and began looking. She took three cute dresses that were perfect for summer off the hanger. One of them fell out of her hand and she bent down to pick it and seen a huge safe with a combination lock on it.

"I hope you found something cause a big black car just pulled up outside," Aunt Nellie said as walked up silently behind Azure.

Azure started screaming loudly running through the house. She peeped out the front window and seen a black and silver Phantom in front. "Ahhhhhhhhhhhhhhhhhh, he didn't even wait for me to call him. Oh, my God!"

Chapter 6

Azure sat across from King with her head down. Her hands were in her lap and she was twiddling her thumbs. She was trying not to make eye contact with him. She felt like a preteen girl, every time she locked eyes with him, she would start blushing. She couldn't believe that he just popped up at her house without calling her. He obviously had started to do a little research on her. She knew that she was going to have to do the same.

Azure was tough and she had a hard knock life from the very beginning, but she still was a one-woman army. After doing those five years in the federal penitentiary, she learned early that there was no such thing as being paranoid. Her intuition was a gift from God.

She had honed her skills and was now using it more. She didn't have a sixth sense, she had a seventh sense and it saved her ass all those years behind bars.

They were sitting on the patio of Infusion Bistro about to have brunch. She had rushed and put on one of Aunt Nellie's long skirts and made it into a halter dress by pulling it over her breast. Azure then put on a chunky western belt and threw on some short cowboy boots. The clothes didn't make her; she made the clothes and she had to admit that as she looked out the floor length mirror before she walked out of her bedroom, she looked damn good.

"I'm sorry bout that Lil' mama. I had to take that call." King had been thinking about her since he laid eyes on her last night. He immediately started asking around to find out if she was indeed Maximillion's woman.

"Business is business, Mustafa. I totally understand. Thank you again for all those beautiful roses. My aunt was on the phone with your grandmother when I left out of the house telling her about how her charming grandson had just filled her house to the brim with all kinds of exotic flowers." Azure was bubbling over on the inside. This was her first time alone in a man's company in five years.

"Oh Lawd, I better get my assistant to go head and send Big Mama some because she can be jealous. She is going to call me later and ask me where her roses are. She is a trip. But that is my baby and I wouldn't trade that lady for anything in the world," King Mustafa said, staring deeply into her eyes, flashing his signature smile. He texted his personal assistant to send his grandmother a dozen roses everyday for the next week. His grandmother was his pride and joy. She raised him and he gave her credit for who and what he was today.

Azure seemed to be getting warmer by the minute as she sat in front of him. His gaze was so intensely focused on her that she still felt it on her when she had broken eye contact. She knew she was flushed, she could feel the heat in her cheeks.

Being in his presence made her miss Maximillion even more. But Maximillion wasn't here and Mustafa was and he might be her key to getting Maximillion out. She just had to play her cards right.

The wheels in her head were turning and as soon as Mustafa reached across the table and grabbed her hand in his, her pussy started to throb.

She closed her eyes and said a silent prayer. *"Please heavenly father, don't let me lose focus on my plan. Don't let my vulnerability get the best of me and please do not let me give this man any sex before he earned it."* Azure laughed to herself as she crossed her legs tightly under the table. At least she was being realistic. She knew that she was indeed going to have sex with Mustafa. She just didn't want to give it up so soon. She had to start doing her research on him as soon as she got home and she knew the first person she had to start with was Aunt Nellie and the second person would be Rocky.

"What's got you smirking? You scared to give me a full smile? I will take that little smirk for now; it is only just the beginning. If I can't do nothing else, I can definitely keep a smile on that beautiful face of yours," King Mustafa said, confidently.

She couldn't do anything to stop the smile that quickly spread across her face. She knew she might have a little trouble on her hands because despite her first impression of him, he wasn't as bad as she thought he was. Azure quickly grabbed the menu to peruse it as she tried to take the focus off this man in front of her.

The waitress approached the table and took their order and quickly departed. She sensed a familiarity between her and Mustafa. She looked up at him and said, "You know her or something?"

"Or something." He quickly grabbed her hand again and began to trace the lines on the underside of her hand with his manicured fingers.

"I got a feeling, you might have a lot of or somethings floating around this city. " Azure snatched her hand away from his a little more forcefully than she intended.

She pushed away a tendril of hair that was tickling the side of her face and put her hand back inside of his upturned palm across the table and smiled so that he wouldn't think that she was being funny.

He looked into the most beautiful set of eyes that he'd ever seen and knew right then that he wanted to possess her for himself. "You know I can read palms right?" He looked down and started to talk.

Chills went down her spine as he traced her lines and told her some things that made the hair on the back of her neck stand up. Azure was happy when the waitress returned with their food. She was thankful for the distraction as he dug in hungrily. Her eyes rolled in the back of her head as she devoured the red velvet waffle with cream cheese drizzle.

Chapter 7:

Azure had not talked to Rocky since she'd seen him at 'Luxurious' the night of his birthday party. She had been hoping that she would have heard from him the next day, but she hadn't.

The only time she really had to herself was in the morning when she went on her five-mile run and at night when Mustafa dropped her off. He told her that he wasn't putting any pressure on her, but he wanted her to spend her every waking moment with him and that was exactly what she had been doing.

She looked at her g-shock and it was almost seven a.m. She had slept late. She didn't get in to after two this morning. Her body was telling her to lie back down and that was exactly what she planned on doing as she rolled over and pulled the cover over her head.

The doorbell started to ring just as she was getting back comfortable under the covers. Azure threw the covers off, growled low and hopped out of bed.

"Ughhhh, who in the fuck comes to someone's house before the sun even comes up?"

She rushed to the door because she didn't want to wake up Aunt Nellie, but she noticed that she was already awoke and had beaten her to the door. She had on her housecoat and she was peeking her head out the door and whispering.

Azure laughed to herself as she noticed the little twenty-two-caliber pistol in her hand. Her aunt was trained to go and she had taught her the same.

"Aunt Nellie, who is that this time of the morning? They got to be crazy, its not even eight o' clock yet. I didn't hear the telephone ringing. Obviously, whoever it is don't have any damn home training." Once she seen that her aunt was equipped with what she liked to call her little peashooter, she turned and headed back to her bedroom.

Fatt Mama pushed Aunt Nellie to the side and walked in the door when she heard Azure's voice. She had been home well over a month and she had yet to reach out. That was why she had come this early. She knew she was bound to catch her at home if she came this early. She had stopped by over a dozen times and even when Azure's Benz was outside; she was still told that she wasn't there.

"Girl it's me, you are never here I've been coming by damn near every other day to see my right hand. Girl, give me a hug. I missed the hell out of you."

Azure recognized the voice instantly and her face instantly went into a grimace as she seen Fatt Mama coming toward her looking completely different. She had a jet-black weave flowing down her back, her make up was perfect and she was fine. She had some plastic surgery done.

She was no longer fat; she was just thick in all the right places. Her humongous stomach was gone, so were the breast that were just as huge. Fatt Mama had done a total make over. She didn't even dress the same.

She had replaced her Polo for some designer duds and her Airmax for Christian Louboutin. But what caught Azure totally off guard were the blue contact lenses in her eyes. It then dawned on her as she looked at what used to be her closest friend and confidante up and down; she was trying to be her.

"Bestie, I thought that I would've been the first person you contact when you touched down. I didn't even know you were coming home, but then you come home and go underground. You know I was supposed to have you a big celebration when you touched down. It ain't too late though, I promise. We are going to have the biggest party at Luxurious." Fatt Mama twirled the long weave around her finger nervously as she leaned up against the wall.

Azure took a deep breath. It was taking everything in her not to go off. She was shaking on the inside as she bit her lower lip trying to think of what to say. She had to play it cool. She couldn't let Fatt Mama know that she knew some of the shit that she had did to her.

"Girl, I was so messed up. I've just been shut up in this house or I go and exercise at the park. I'm just trying to get myself together. So much has changed out here, you feel me cuz. I'm not sure of anything anymore, not even myself. But enough about me, you look awesome, I mean really fantastic. I like this transformation." Azure wasn't lying. She did think that she looked awesome; she looked just like her.

"Really cuz, I'm so happy that you do. It cost a lot, but it was worth it. I'm so happy with myself finally. Dr. Curves worked a miracle on me. Throw on some clothes; I got a little play money. Let me take you to breakfast and grab you a few things from our spot "Phipps Plaza". We got a lot of catching up to do." Fatt Mama seemed to relax after Azure gave her approval on her transformation.

She had been waiting for the time when she would be face to face with Azure. It seemed that it came sooner than later, but that it is okay. She was about to work this situation.

"Okay girl, let me run to the back and slip on something right quick."

She went into her bedroom and sat on the bed and exhaled deeply. When you are genuinely beautiful on the inside, it doesn't matter if you are in a paper bag you will be noticed. She was about to prove that to Fatt Mama today. Azure threw on a pair of True Religion jeans that she cut into short shorts. They were five years old and fit

40

her really loose. They didn't fit her any of her curves because they were at least four sizes too big.

She threw on a Mickey Mouse T-shirt that she had picked up at Target. Pulled her hair in a messy ponytail on top of her head. Got the long matching Mickey Mouse socks out of her chest of drawers and put on the Air Jordan's that Mustafa had bought them the other day when they were together.

He had basically taken her shopping every day when he picked her up. She came home late every night loaded with bags from all over. He was beyond generous and sweet. Totally different from the person that she met in the club on his birthday. Azure finished her look with a long sleeved plaid True Religion shirt that belonged to Maximillion that she tied around her waist and some MAC nude lip glass to her lips.

She was about to grab one of her many vintage Louie bags when her cellphone rang. She grabbed it quickly. It was probably Mustafa calling to tell her good morning. No matter when time he got in the night before, he was always at his desk checking stocks and emails by nine a.m.

This was an unfamiliar number, she started to hit the decline button on her iPhone 5s, but instead she answered it.

"You have a prepaid call from... Maximillion Stevens. Press 5 to accept."

Her knees instantly begin to shake: she sat down on the bed and stared at the phone after she pressed the five. Azure breath seemed to be caught in her chest as it became tight as soon as she heard him say her name.

"Blue, Blue, are you there?" Maximillion said. He had been debating on whether or not to call her for a few days and after he made up his mind that he would call her, he had to get his emotions in check because he had so much inside and all of it was Blue.

The tears poured down her face like a dam had broken and she wiped them away and sniffled as her nose ran. She had been waiting five years to hear his voice. Her voice was caught in her throat as she answered him, "Yes Max, I'm here baby. I'm here."

Azure was hoping that Rocky would get him to call her, but she could never prepare herself for how she felt. She hadn't even heard what he had to say, but just hearing his voice alone filled her with hope.

Hearing her crying made him so vulnerable and he couldn't give her a tongue-lashing. He softened up and exhaled deeply. "I've missed you Beautiful one. I didn't know it was possible to love somebody so much that it hurt. I didn't know it was possible to actually live without your heart. I didn't know it was possible to love someone and hate them at the same time. You have broken my heart and my spirit. I never in a million years could believe you of all people would do me like this. Baby, what in the world did I do to you for you to treat me this way?"

Max didn't care who was watching him cry. He had waited a long time to get this off of his chest.

Hearing this was like a knife straight to the heart and she couldn't talk. She just cried and cried. It seemed like all of the pain she had been holding inside was finally coming out. The beating, the miscarriage, being abandoned, losing everything especially him it was all coming out through her tears that she could no longer keep silent. She wept aloud for everything that they were supposed to be and everything that they were.

He couldn't bear to hear her crying like this. It was tearing him up inside and he couldn't even get his thoughts together because he was actually visualizing her with the tears coming from her eyes, her face red from crying so hard. Max wanted to wrap her in his arms, but he couldn't.

This was not what he expected. He wanted to cuss her out for how she left him for dead, but he couldn't hurt her with his words. Because at the end of the day, this was the only woman who he ever loved. This is the only woman who carried his child inside of them. Azure was indeed the love of his life and there was no denying that.

There was a knock on her bedroom door. Azure had totally forgotten that Fatt Mama was in the living room waiting on her. Her plan was to play green to everything with Fatt Mama, so she wasn't going to reveal that she had even had contact with Max.

"Max, things went so wrong and I'm sorry. Don't you ever doubt for one second that I haven't thought about you every day when I wake up and every night that I go to sleep since the day when we were ripped apart. You will always be my king and there is nothing and no one in the world who can stop that. Do you hear me?" Azure heard the pain in his voice, when he sniffled; she knew that he was crying, too.

"Yes."

"You have sixty seconds left," the automated recording interrupted her.

"Baby, please call me this evening. I'm about to head to the mall and out to eat with Fatt Mama," Azure said quickly before the call was disconnected.

"Keep the grass cut low, that's a big ass snake, Ma'." Max said as the call was disconnected.

Chapter 8:

They stepped out of Fatt Mama's Jaguar F-type in Phipps Plaza valet. Azure had been quiet the entire ride over. She was sizing Fatt Mama up as she ran her mouth telling her stuff that had been going on since she been gone. Azure barely replied and when she did it was with short answers. All she continued to hear was Max's words before he got off the phone replaying in her head. *"That's a big ass snake ma."*

"You didn't tell me what you think of the car cuz. I was the first bitch in the city with this motherfucka. All these regular ass bitches riding these Camaros, Challengers, and Chargers. I had to show them bitches how it supposed to be done," Fatt Mama said proudly as she strutted into the mall's entrance.

Azure instantly turned her head in Fatt Mama's direction with a snap of the neck. "Girl gone. I would ride the hell out of a Camaro. I like the Challenger and the Charger is cool, too. You was just a regular bitch yourself not too long ago. When you started working with me, you didn't even have a car, you used the junkies in the neighborhood for rides or caught the bus. I helped you get your first car from the police auction. You rode the wheels off of that little Impala. Then you moved up and got a

Pontiac Grand Prix before I left. Now you on your high horse, I bet you pay a note on this motherfucker. If something happened to you tomorrow this car will be gone. Don't get beside yourself honey. I know the real you. When you got some titles in your hand, then you can pop a little shit. Until then, pipe down Fatt Mama, that shit ain't cute."

"Damn cuz, it seem like I struck a nerve. You never have been a regular bitch. I'm not talking bout you. It's gonna take for you to be out in the city to see what is going on, and how these hoes have changed up." Fatt Mama was trying to calm Azure down after she spazzed on her. She knew her temper was uncontrollable.

Azure thought to herself that she didn't need to be out in the city to see how hoes change up. She was looking at a hoe who had did a total three sixty.

"All I'm saying is humble yourself. You weren't born into this shit and you are not getting it legal. This shit could be taken away from you in the blink of an eye, look what happened to me. God knows everybody ain't built the same." She reached to get her ringing cellphone from her purse. It was King. She immediately started smiling. She held up one finger in Fatt Mama's face as she walked in the opposite direction to have some privacy.

"Hey, how is my baby girl doing? I'm on my way to come and get you, so be ready when I pull up. I got a surprise for you," King said, jovially. Every night when he dropped her off, he couldn't wait until the next morning

46

to pick her up. He had to admit when he first seen her he was all for the visual. She was drop dead gorgeous, but the icing on the cake was that she was an intellectual and a free thinker.

She made him think of so many things in a different way. They had yet to be intimate. He wanted to be a complete gentleman with her, so he was cool with waiting on her. Plus he could get pussy when he couldn't get anything to eat. They were on a glorious mind fuck.

"Hey you, I'm good, I'm not at home. My cousin came over early this morning before I could even go for my run and kidnapped me. I will call you when I get home." Azure ended the call; she had to admit that liked the way things were flowing between the two of them. She was enjoying it, but she knew that all the fun and games were going to have to stop, especially after the phone call this morning from Max. Playtime was over, now it was time to get to work on doing whatever was necessary to get Max home.

"Girl, who was that? They got you smiling from ear to ear. Come on now you can tell me. This is cuz here," Fatt Mama said trying to figure out whom Azure had just gotten off the phone with.

Azure didn't say anything. She just smiled harder and tucked her phone back into her purse. She thought to herself, that is why she will never tell this bitch anymore of her secrets, she will never know the inner workings of

Azure Knight. She wasn't her 'mini-me' she was her 'bigger me'.

"Okay, I guess we keeping secrets now, that's cool. By the way, I like your lil' get up. That is real cute," Fatt Mama said as she walked ahead of Azure into the Gucci store.

Azure shook her head. She learned a long time ago about a bitch that sizes up your accomplishments. Even though her and King had been coming in and out of Phipps that was one place that she had not been. This used to be her and Max's second home. They had the head salesperson Julie on speed dial and she had them on hers. Tears almost sprang from her eyes, but she tried her hardest to hold them back. She wouldn't let Fatt Mama see her cry or show her any sign of vulnerability for that matter. All this was only going to make her go harder.

Fatt Mama walked in flexing her muscle as she flipped her hair over her shoulder. Her confidence was on ten as she sauntered around the store looking at shoes and purses. She knew that Azure was feeling some kind of way because she wasn't able to do these types of things anymore. She picked up a royal blue high heel and matching clutch and turned around to find the salesperson.

"Blue, Darling how good to see you." Julie the salesperson walked out from the back of the store.

Azure looked up from where she was sitting on the bench in the direction of Julie bewildered. How did she know it was her? She had her head held down and she didn't even look the same. She smiled, but quickly stopped when she seen that Julie was talking to Fatt Mama instead.

Her heart started beating extremely fast and she started to perspire. It was taking everything in her not to get up and go and knock Fatt Mama off her feet.

Fatt Mama glanced in Azure's direction and tried to laugh it off. But her nervous laughter didn't hide the fear in her eyes. She knew it was going to happen sooner or later, no one called her Fatt Mama. She was known as Lil Blue or Blue in the streets. In her eyes, Fatt Mama was dead, so Azure better get used to it. She offered to buy Azure something. Maybe that would pacify her. "Yo Cuz, you see anything in here you want?

Azure looked up at Fatt Mama and rolled her eyes. "Might as well, you know a bitch hasn't stepped in Gucci in five years." She stood and walked around the store looking to see what she could get. Whatever it was it was going to be expensive and she dared that fat bitch to say no. She picked up the blue Guccisma Leather Hobo and held it up.

"Are you a stylist? I love your look it is flawless, yet it effortless. You make tomboy seem chic. It's fantastic." Julie smiled at Azure at she looked her up and down.

"Nope, I'm just little old me. What else do you have to go with this bag? Bring everything, it's on my cuz." Although Azure had a wide smile on her face, her blue eyes was shooting daggers at Fatt Mama who smiled pretentiously as she walked around the store looking at items as if she was actually interested in them.

Two men came in the store as Fatt Mama sat on the bench and tried on shoes. "Damn Blue you decide to go shopping this morning, so that is why I didn't get a good morning text."

Azure didn't even look up at the guys, she just shook her head as Julie came over and bought her a wallet, belt and scarf that matched the bag. She was going to get something out of every store that they went into, not because she needed it, or even because she wanted it, but more because this bitch owed her.

"You look so familiar. You say you aren't a stylist, are you perhaps a model? I know I have seen you somewhere. I didn't just see you; we interacted because even your voice sounds familiar. I can't put my finger on it, but it is going to come to me," Julie said before walking over to Fatt Mama and the two guys.

Azure didn't even care to tell her who she was. She was new and improved; she would let Fatt Mama have that whole set up. She had made mistakes in her former life that she couldn't get a do over for.

Chapter 8:

Fatt Mama looked over at Azure sitting in the passenger's seat as they headed back to Aunt Nellie's house. She thought that she was going to spaz out on her after what happened in the Gucci store, so she continued to shower her with gifts to keep her quiet.

She had to admit she didn't feel bad as she probably should have when Azure was away in prison. It was while she was gone that she was able to find herself and improve herself. She no longer was living in Azure's shadow.

"Who were those two guys who took us to lunch? They seemed cool and Ol' Dude seemed to really be digging you, but you was shooting him down." Even though she had formed a deep seeded hate for Fatt Mama she still was just like family and it was easy to fall back into their routine of being a dynamic duo like *Laverne and Shirley', 'Betty and Wilma', 'Cagney and Lacey,' 'Monica and Rachel', 'Meredith and Christina'*.

"Oh, you mean Solo? He calls me all the time asking to take me out and shit, but I continue to turn him down. Today was the first time we actually broke bread together. He's been chasing me for about eight months now. I see him in the club and he will smoke one with me or give me some weed. He will buy me a bottle or let me in his section, but he really is not my type. I'm digging his homeboy. That is who attention that I'm trying to grab. I mean he got a lil' paper to play with and he stay fly, but I'm after bigger fish. You said it yourself earlier, shit can change up for me in the blink of an eye." Fatt Mama snapped her fingers for emphasis.

"But he seems genuine and in this day and age you rarely meet really genuine people, so stop being so mean. Max wasn't on top when I got with him. You seen what he was working with, but he wanted me and he wanted to make me happy. Girl you got to be with somebody whose ultimate goal is to make you happy," Azure said to Fatt Mama. No matter how she felt, she stayed real no matter what.

"Yeah, you're right. But you should see his boss. This man is at the top of the totem pole. He is the epitome of a boss, he calls all the shots and you never see him in the trenches with the troops and his hands never get dirty. He got so many businesses around the city, and he educated. People don't even know that he is one of the major importers of the dope in the city because he is educated and got the businesses. The reason that I know that he is the boss is because of Solo. So to a regular bitch in the street, Solo would be a big catch cause he is the one that is hustling the work. I want the nigga bringing it over, I want King."

"Hurry up and get me home honey. I can't take much more of this shallow shit with you. You have turned into a real monster while I was gone. I don't need that shit rubbing off on me. I'm in a really good space. Let me tell you what attracts and keeps a real man, a bitch that is on her shit. Not a fat ass, not a small waist, not a cute face, not some long weave, not a foreign car, and definitely not having your face in the place all the time.

Real men want substance, and you keep throwing regular bitch around shows that you do not have any. But with what you got going on now, might catch you a real nigga. There is a difference." Azure ended the conversation. She taught her enough along the way, class was out and school was over.

"I see prison has changed you, but I know the real you. How you want me to fuck with the help and you never fucked with the help? Aren't you contradictory?" Fatt Mama said as they pulled up in Aunt Nellie's driveway. She knew that she had spent close to ten racks on Azure in the mall. That was small compared to all that she had made from her teachings and plugs over the years. She felt like this was the least she could do, although she didn't intend to spend that much money.

Azure had a long drawn out sermon she could preach, but she knew that Fatt Mama wouldn't get the half and didn't deserve the quarter. She hoped out before Fatt Mama could and rushed to her trunk to try and get all the bags without her help. Even though it was the evening, she knew that she was going to have to go for a run to clear her mind and meditate about the day.

She got out and Azure already had all the bags and was struggling to close the trunk. Fatt Mama did it and started to follow her up the walkway to the house. But she was stopped in her tracks by Azure.

"People change, some for the better, some for the worst. My soul aged in that prison, my heart broke in that prison. You don't know the person standing before you and to be honest, I don't want you to get to know her. You might try to rob a bank to become her. I appreciate the little gifts Little Blue." Azure walked up the steps and leaned on the doorbell. She didn't even turn around to look at Fatt Mama.

Aunt Nellie rushed to door, she had been looking at her wristwatch off and on during the day wondering when her baby was gonna get back home. She opened the door and Azure was loaded down with bags.

This was a daily occurrence with her, maybe shopping was her therapy; at least she wasn't spending her money.

"Girl, if your ass bring one more damn bag in this house I don't know what I'm going to do. This was nice of Fatt Mama, I know she sure missed you when you were gone."

"Tuh, yeah right. She missed me so much she became me. I know you wearing glasses and all, but you can't tell me that you have missed her transformation into my little prototype. Do you know that she is telling people that her name is Blue? Are you fucking kidding me? She stole my style, had plastic surgery to improve her physical appearance, she wears her hair like I used to, dresses like I used to, and even has blue contact lenses. You know you could have prepared me for this. I swear you can knock me over with a feather, this day has taken a lot out of me." Azure headed to her bedroom, but Aunt Nellie was on her heels.

"Yes, I noticed the changes, they say that imitation is the sincerest form of flattery. You know that she always looked up to you." Aunt Nellie sat on Azure's bed and started to ramble through the shopping bags as Azure changed into her running gear.

"I've heard the same, but it's kinda scary. I needed this day. Even though it has been a little rough, it's exactly what I needed. I've faced the worst part; it is only going to get better. I was afraid to talk to Max and I've conquered that. I was afraid to see Fatt Mama because I thought I wouldn't be able to contain my anger toward her and I conquered that. Now I can focus on what I need to focus on. And that is bringing my man home and getting me my own money." Azure laced up her Asics running shoes and grabbed a hoody before turning to head back out the door.

"I'm sorry today was rough on you. But I know you are strong baby girl. You are my super hero. Enjoy your time with King. You don't need to be trying to do all that shit that got you in trouble in the first place. Let him provide for you. He is head over heels already, his grandmother told me." Aunt Nellie had been watching Azure hard, she didn't want her being around Fatt Mama cause her to get any ideas in her head to go back in business with them Nigerians.

She was hoping that King would sweep her off her feet so she wouldn't be so caught up in putting her life on the line to get Max released or putting her life on hold until he came home.

Chapter 9:

Azure sat on the bed, the sun was about to come up and King had just dropped her off again. Several days had passed since she talked to Max. She had been anticipating his call, but in the meantime she had been trying to get her thoughts together.

The more time she spent with Mustafa, the more she found herself liking him. He was not letting up with his pursuit of her. He made it known that he wanted her badly. He was constantly showering her with gifts and giving her all the attention that she could want.

After the day out with Fatt Mama, she knew that she had to step her game up. There was no way she was about to let her prototype was outshine her. Her endgame was for Max to be home and back on the throne and for her to have her boutique.

She couldn't let her feelings of hate for Fatt Mama stop that or the increasing feelings that were growing for Mustafa knock her off her feet. Azure rubbed her hands together deviously before she jumped off the bed. She hollered out, "That's it!"

Hustling was in her DNA, and she was a fast learner. She was not trying to get back into the white-collar shit because the feds were waiting for her to slip up. Azure needed to spend some time with Rocky. He would be able to school her on who the movers and shakers were in the game now. But from what Fatt Mama said Mustafa was a key player. She knew couldn't go to him on nothing business related. But she needed her own money to make her dreams a reality. If she was nothing else, she was a go-getter.

Azure dropped to the floor beside her bed and started to do some push-ups in her bra and panties. She was not going to sleep, she needed to plan and she found that when she was exercising her thoughts flowed clearly. Being that she was a natural leader and a finesser, she could get people to do things that they wouldn't usually do.

Fatt mama would be perfect to be in on this, she could be her face as she played the background. She had to watch Mustafa a lot closer because she was with him everyday and she didn't see any tale tell signs that he was a major distributor. That is what level she needed to be on, she must play the background. She needed some puppets whose strings she could pull because nothing could ever fall back on her.

Aunt Nellie opened the door and seen Azure lying on her back doing sit-ups and crunches. It was five thirty in the morning. *This girl has lost her mind.* Instead of closing the door and heading back to her bedroom down the hall, she walked in the room and sat down on her bed.

"Okay, what is bothering you? You up exercising like you in the Army boot camp. Talk to me."

She was pouring sweat as she got up and started doing jumping jacks while her Aunt looked at her like she was crazy. Azure did two hundred jumping jacks and then started to do some squats while her aunt stared at her in amazement.

All kind of thoughts was racing through her head as she felt her adrenaline pumping. She stopped and looked at her aunt. "Why you staring at me like that little lady? You act like you never seen someone exercising."

"Not like that honey, girl you are a beast. You act like you training for something." Aunt Nellie moved over so Azure could sit down on the bed beside her.

"I am training, I'm training for life. You cooking me full course meals and Mustafa taking me out to five star restaurants everyday will have me 'round her looking like I need to be called Fatt Mama. Plus I like the way I feel when I'm exercising."

"Speaking of Fatt Mama, she came by yesterday when you were gone with your little boyfriend. She was talking bout what happened that day she took you shopping. She said that you didn't even act like you were appreciative," Aunt Nellie said to Azure.

"Now, I told the bitch thank you, I don't know what else I supposed to do. I know she didn't expect me to kiss her ass. See I'm not bout to get into this with you because you don't know the entire story." Azure hopped up off the bed, and headed to her bathroom to shower.

Aunt Nellie didn't take that as a cue to leave, she instead followed her into the bathroom. "You still haven't told me what is bothering you? What can I do to fix this?" She raised Azure, she knew her like the back of her own hand. She could feel that she was in turmoil. She thought things were getting better since she started dating King Mustafa. She was no longer moping around the house with a long face, her every other word was no longer Max.

"You know those dreams that I had, I still want them to come true. I still want my boutique, I still want children, and I still want to be Max's wife. That is my happily ever after. I want that, I deserve that. Every move that I make right now is for that. That is my endgame." Azure grabbed the towel, wrapped it around her and walked around her aunt, who was standing in the doorway.

"Things don't always happen in the order that you want them to or the way that you plan, but if it's meant to be, it will happen baby. I don't want you to give up on your dreams, especially of your boutique. I look at television and you dress better than all those girls that I see on them reality shows filmed down here. Maybe your boyfriend can help you with your business, after all he is a big business man around town." Aunt Nellie knew that if

Azure opened her boutique that the sky would be the limit.

"I enjoy Mustafa's company, he is much more than I expected when I met him, but he is not my boyfriend, he is a friend. I'm not trying to get too attached because Max is coming home soon. I actually need to quit spending so much time with Mustafa and try to focus my energy on making some money, so I can start living my dreams. These girls in Atlanta got it fucked up Auntie, they concentrating on being a millionaire's girl, I'm concentrating on being the girl with millions. I gotta make a way. I've already been working on my business plan." Azure went over to her chest of drawers and pulled out a notebook and cat suit. She handed Aunt Nellie the notebook and she dried off and put on clothes.

She opened the notebook and started reading what Azure had written and she flipped through page after page of plans and sketches. *So this is what she had been working on when she was shut up in the room.* "Girl this is what you been doing, this looks fantastic, what do you need me to do?"

"I need you to put your name on it," Azure said seriously despite the huge smile that spread across her face when she heard her favorite girl let her know she was in.

"So, you got the money for start up already?" Aunt Nellie knew this girl could work magic when it came to them men, well really when it came to anyone. Azure always had them eating out of her hands. She probably had called up some of her old connects. She gained a lot of respect on the street because she didn't snitch on anyone; she did her time and didn't ask anybody for anything.

"Nope, I don't have two pennies to rub together. First of all, will you put your name on it? If you do that I know everything will just flow. With your credit we can get a loan, and I'm going to start pulling a few cards and calling in some favors." Azure mood had changed dramatically she was amped up.

Chapter 10:

After her very eventful morning with Aunt Nellie, she knew the first person that she had to talk to was Rocky. She agreed to meet him for breakfast in both of their favorite place to eat. "Thumbs Up" used to be where her, Max, and Rocky would eat breakfast at least two or three times a week. Since she been gone, they had opened one on the Westside right off of Bankhead, which coincidently was right down the street from Rocky's condo.

Azure walked in and she instantaneously felt all eyes on her. She blushed and looked around for Rocky, who happened to be ducked off sitting all the way in the back of the restaurant. Used to getting attention, she held her head high as she strutted through the restaurant in her Christian Louboutin Tina Suede stiletto boots to the last booth where Rocky was smiling at her.

"Your lil' ass always knew how to make a grand entrance. Good to see you sis. I thought I would have heard from you before now, but hey now is better than never." Rocky looked at the new version of Azure and he had to admit that he liked it. She had toned her look down, but in that her natural beauty shined through and you would think that the ugly scar on her face would take away from her look. It actually gave her face character.

"Whatever bro, I thought you would have called me so we could link up. I know you have talked to Max; he only called that one time. I told him to call me back later, but he didn't." Azure had been puzzled to why Max had not called her anymore since they reconnected.

"Imma be honest, the streets talk and if they are talking, you know that he knows. Everybody knows that you are kicking it heavy with King Mustafa. He asked me about it and I told him that night that is who you came in the club with. I can't lie to my brother, for nobody." Rocky stopped talking when the waitress approached the table to take their order.

They both placed their orders and remained silent. Azure pondered over what Rocky had just said. She didn't care how much Mustafa had going for himself; she didn't want to be known as his girl. They were dating and she was enjoying his company, but she kept her eyes on the prize. He was just a pawn on her board. Max was her king and he was her endgame. She told Rocky all of this and he looked her in her eyes and he seen the sincerity of what she was saying.

"Be careful sis, somebody is bound to get hurt. Don't play with that man's feelings. Niggas react differently to things these days. I've been looking at the news, they going out bad bout these bitches, they killing them and killing themselves, too. You can't play with a motherfucker's heart," Rocky said remembering the pain he heard in Max's voice when he asked him if he knew whether or not Azure was fucking round with King Mustafa.

"I'm not trying to hurt anyone. That is why I'm focusing on getting my own bread and making my own dreams coming true. I got too much inside me to just be a nigga's arm candy. I need your help. I'm going to open my boutique. I need to get Max a new lawyer, so he can go up for an appeal. I don't want that nigga, I want my nigga." Azure greedily dug into food as soon as it was placed before her.

"Sounds like you got a plan, you know I'm all in. But let me tell you this first, my money ain't flowing like it was. I have downsized a lot. It seemed like since that big robbery a few months ago, I haven't been able to bounce back like I thought I would. It takes money to make money and shit right now my money ain't flowing. I don't even have a spot. I'm strictly working off my phone. You know that is so unlike me sis. I always kept a honeycomb hideout." Azure was like his sister, so he wasn't afraid to tell her that times had gotten hard for him lately. She would never judge him.

"You are alive, you still got your health and your strength and you are of sound mind. That is all that matters. As long as you got those things you can get back on top. We might be able to help each other. I can put my hands on some money, but I need to make it grow. I just

66

got out of the feds; so you know it's a lot of things that are off limits. I'm a female; I can't be doing a lot of shit by myself. I need you in on this shit Rocky."

After Aunt Nellie told Azure that she could give her some money and she would sign for a loan, her mind went into overdrive. She was going to have to go back to the basics, 'Trap or die"

"Sis, what do you have in mind? I know if the both of us put our heads together we can damn sure make that lil' bit of money grow. I'm with it, just tell me your plan." Rocky was hungrier than he thought. He wolfed his omelet down in record timing.

"It's a good amount to give us a running start. I need to do some work and we got to get us a spot in our old neighborhood; I prefer a house. We are bout to go back to 2004, when we were busting folk heads with the best of the best."

"A spot? Some work? Sis, you trying to start trapping?" Rocky didn't know what he thought she had in mind but it definitely wasn't this. He remembered when Azure and Max first got together and he always sent her away whenever they would start working so she wouldn't be exposed to it. But in the end, she was right there with them weighing shit, cutting shit, bagging up shit.

"I got the money, and I got the know how, but I need you to be the man on the battlefield cause I got too much to lose. You will talk to all the soldiers and be the go to man. I can't be caught down bad with this. Can you do this bro?" Azure knew that it was possible for her to play the background. Mustafa did it so well. She wanted to be known as the boutique owner, Max's girl, not a drug dealer.

"I got ya, I got ya. How much money are we talking bout right now?" His eyes lit up, he had been patiently waiting on his time to come back around and it look like Azure was about to help him get back right.

"I got fifty thousand right now, but the Nigerians owe me big time. I didn't rat them out and I didn't even ask them to feed me while I was gone. I know Peebo will give me whatever I ask for." Azure knew the code of the streets and she stuck to them no matter what the circumstances were. If she was nothing else she was definitely thorough.

The wheels instantly started turning in Rocky's head as he thought about what he needed to do and whom he needed to call. When Max got locked up, he started fucking with Gigi and then she got messed up, he started messing with Whyte and his boys, but then they got banged up. He tried to think of whom he knew that was eating in the streets right now. He said the name out loud. "Solo"

"What about Solo?" Azure said to Rocky, as she got ready to get up and leave. She put four ten-dollar bills on the table to take care of their breakfast.

"You know Solo?" Rocky asked with his eyebrow raised.

"Yes, I met him when me and Fatt Mama went shopping. He likes her and he treated us to lunch at the Tavern when we were out shopping at Phipps Plaza," Azure said to answer his question.

"Fatt Mama, don't you mean Lil' Blue." Rocky got up from the booth laughing hysterically. He had not gotten a chance to talk to Azure about her prototype's transformation.

"I swear, I almost died when I seen her, but when I heard her responding by my name, it had to be an angel in heaven keeping me from swinging on her in the middle of Phipps Plaza. Max told me she was a snake, in fact those were his last words to me when we spoke on the phone last week." Azure and Rocky walked out the door of the restaurant; she hugged him and told him to call her. Rocky headed in the direction of a 2014 black on black Chevy Corvette.

Chapter 10:

Things got into motion faster than she thought that they would. Rocky seemed to be waiting for this opportunity that he jumped off the porch with both feet. Today was the day that he was moving into the duplex on Hollywood Road. Azure was happy that the other side was vacant. She stopped by to see him before she headed home. She was proud of all of her accomplishments this week.

He came to the door with a wife beater on; he now had tattooed sleeves on both of his arms. She remembered when he got his first tattoo. He had a blunt in his mouth and his cellphone up to his ear listening to someone talking to him very loudly on the other end. Rocky ended the call and took a deep pull of the blunt and then reached it out to Azure.

"Boy, I don't smoke or drink anymore. I'm new and improved inside out," she said proudly turning her nose up at the smell. She remembered her and Max used to get blazed.

"That's good sis, but I need this shit to cope. I ain't lying." Rocky blew various size circles in the air as put the blunt out in the ashtray on the kitchen counter.

"You didn't waste no time. That is what I'm talking bout. Have you talked to your people about product yet?" Azure said as she looked around. She had been distancing herself from Mustafa. She was spending a lot of time at the central library researching for her business. She decided to enroll in school, as well.

She knew that running a business was going to take a lot out of her, but she felt like she didn't want to half ass nothing and her going to school to get a degree wouldn't hurt one bit. An idle mind was a devil's workshop. Its amazing that everything Max wanted her to do when he was out here on the street as a top earner was what she wanted to do now that he was gone.

"I have been scouting, I got my ear to the streets. We need to get our hands on some of everything, but it has to be top quality. This needs to be a one-stop shop, like Wal-Mart. It's not like when you went in. Cocaine and weed still sells, but its other shit out here to get some real money with like heroin, prescription pills, lean, and mollies. These days everybody is on some type of drug," Rocky said as he slipped his Armani Exchange t-shirt on over his tank top.

"I feel you, but you've to got be careful. I'm thinking positive, but we might need to stick to what we know for sure. When you start messing with heroin, and them scripts that's straight to fed. We don't even want to be on them folks radar."

"You just worry about the plans for your boutique and the lawyer for Max, I got this. Soon as I lock in with a good connect, I'mma hit you up to get the cash. Matter of fact, I'm bout to meet Solo right now over at *Gigi's Pleasure Chest.*"

She remembered the days of being the only girl with Max and the crew when they hit up all the stripper spots. Those things used to excite her, she used to love being on the scene with the flyest shit, stepping out the flyest whip while with the most bossed up clique.

Azure was proud of her growth as a person. That was one reason why she wasn't so bitter about going to prison, it made her into a better person, but she was fucked up about how her one and only supposed to friend did her when she was locked up.

"Okay well just holler at me when you need me, I will be around." She walked toward the door as her phone started to vibrate in her bag. She pulled it out and it was Mustafa. She pressed ignore and sent him a message that said 'In a meeting, will call you later.' Azure got in her car and headed home. She had some brainstorming to do.

The black phantom was in her parking spot in the driveway, so she didn't even bother pulling in. She instead parked in front of the house, so she wouldn't block him in. Azure took a deep breath before she got out of her truck, stretched, and then hiked up the small hill that was in Aunt Nellie's front yard.

She laughed as she got to the top; she turned around and jumped up and down like Sylvester Stallone did in Rocky when he got to the top of the steps. She knew that Mustafa was going to show up eventually. After all, she had been avoiding him like the plague for almost a week. She took a deep breath and walked into the house.

"There you are. I thought that I was going to have to put out an all points bulletin on my beautiful Blue." Mustafa was seated in the recliner with a teacup in his hand. He looked right at home in the living room talking to Aunt Nellie, who was smiling from ear to ear.

To hear him call her the same thing Max called her sent a chill down her spine. It seemed like the more she was around this nigga, the more she missed her nigga. He was one of the reasons why she had submersed herself in making her own dreams come true, that and the fact she wanted Max to be proud of her. Her goal was to be much more than some man's arm candy.

"Greetings Mustafa, how are you? I see you are working your magic. You got my Auntie in here smiling and blushing like a teenager." Azure sat down on the love seat right next Aunt Nellie.

"He actually came by earlier to take you out to lunch and I told him this is the time that you have been getting in all week. I let him know that you were busy working on your business plans for your boutique and that you had just enrolled in the university. He such a sweetheart, he went out and bought you something special and made it back just in time for dinner." Aunt Nellie really liked King Mustafa. He was good for Azure plus he wasn't a drug dealer either.

"Ohhhhhhh, really!" Azure looked at her with a side eye, she felt like she was being set up. She hated the fact that her aunt was telling her business, even if it was for bragging rights. She knew that she was a private person.

"My corporation has a scholarship fund, we supply full rides. We also provide assistance to minorities looking to start small businesses. Let me know if you are interested," King Mustafa said smiling lustfully at Azure. He couldn't even deny that he missed being around her everyday. She was like his sunshine on a rainy day.

He had been racking his brain to see what he could have possibly done wrong. He breathed a sigh of relief when he found out that she had actually been busy instead of just ignoring him.

"Full rides, yeah I bet you do." Azure laughed at his comment. Aunt Nellie looked back and forth between them cheesing like a Cheshire cat before she got up to go to the kitchen.

As soon as Aunt Nellie was out of the room, King Mustafa stood up and went to sit beside Azure. He grabbed her hand in his and put it to his lips. He kissed it gently before turning to face her.

"I have missed you so much, you had me feeling some type of way. All I have been getting is short text messages from you all week. You can be honest now that your aunt is no longer in the room. Did I do something wrong?"

In between her legs started to throb as soon as his soft full lips touched the back of her hand. She really didn't want to look up into his eyes, because just the sound of his deep baritone was making her weak. The sincerity in his concern was genuine and she felt it. "It is not you; you know that I just came home from prison. I got to make a new way, for the next day. My light has not been put out; it was just dimmed for a while. I still have my entire life ahead of me and me having a registered number with the federal bureau of prisons is not going to deter me. I enjoyed spending time with you, you have been wonderful, but I gotta get myself together." She finally looked up and made eye contact with him and she almost melted into the cushion on the sofa.

Mustafa reached over and grabbed her chin to turn her face to his. He leaned in and kissed her deeply. The fire spread between the both of them as their tongues danced in each other's mouth.

Instead of tensing up like she usually did whenever he kissed her or rubbed on her, Azure leaned into him. He wrapped his large arms around her; she was hard and soft at the same time. He inhaled her scent; she smelled like heaven. He wanted that scent to linger in his nostrils forever.

Aunt Nellie walked into the room and she honestly didn't expect to see them on the loveseat making out like teenagers. She cleared her throat and said, "You young folks go wash up for dinner." She turned around smiling from ear to ear as she went back into the kitchen to fix their plates.

Azure got up slowly, her legs felt like spaghetti under her when she stood. She had not tongue kissed in five years. Her loins were on fire, she wanted to run to her bedroom and finish the job. She exhaled loudly and shook her head as she looked over at Mustafa, who was blushing despite his dark skin. He had gotten her hot and bothered and she honestly didn't want to stop. Right now, she wanted to be touched by this man.

Mustafa got up and followed behind Azure watching her perfect curves as they moved in front of her. He wanted her more now than he ever wanted her. His penis was hard in his pants and he knew that when he went into the restroom that he was going to have to readjust himself to hide his growing bulge.

He leaned up against the wall and waited for her to finish washing up. He thought to himself, when exactly did he start to fall in love with this girl, that was not what he intended to happened.

Chapter 11:

Azure had learned a long time ago to *never say never;* because history had showed her that she would have to eat those nevers. The sun peaked over the top of the dark curtains in the Grand Suite of the Melia hotel. She rubbed her eyes and tried to roll over, but she couldn't because Mustafa literally had her pinned down.

His long, thick muscular legs were on top of her legs and his long arms were wrapped around her. Azure exhaled deeply and was thankful that she didn't have to use the restroom. She snuggled deeper into him and replayed last night's events in her head.

Aunt Nellie had cooked a Sunday dinner on a Friday night. She knew exactly what she was doing. Beef Pot Roast, Roasted vegetables, Collard Greens, Macaroni and Cheese, black eyed peas, rice, fresh fried corn, ho-cakes, and sweet tea with her famous Strawberry Cake in the middle of the table.

They said the grace and ate the meal in silence, all you heard was the silverware hitting the plates, and the chewing and moans that comes with eating soul food. The sexual tension was in the air and Aunt Nellie knew it. She cleared her throat, "Azure, did you like your surprise? I know that it will definitely come in handy with everything that you have going on."

She looked at her aunt with the side eye again. This little lady was a trip, she knew how to push and pull all the right buttons. "Yes I liked my surprise. It took my breath away." Azure looked over at Mustafa, who was blushing again. He stood up from the table.

"My breath is taken away every time I'm in your presence Beautiful Blue and it seems I can't think straight either because I totally forgot to give you what I got for you today." He walked out of the dining room.

"Ol' lady will you stop your stuff? Jesus Christ stop applying so much pressure. You are just going to throw me on the man." Azure laughed at her aunt's persistence.

"I seen you damn near on top of him on that loveseat. I didn't have anything to do with all that bumping and grinding and kissing that you guys were just doing in that other room." Aunt Nellie got quiet when Mustafa came back in the room carrying the box.

"I went and got you this after I came over earlier and your aunt told me about your plans. This will come in handy with school and business." He handed Azure the MacBook Pro 13inch laptop computer and waited for her reaction.

Azure's eyes lit up like the Macy's Christmas tree as she jumped up from her seat shaking the table. She rushed and gave Mustafa a hug. She needed a computer and had actually been doing research on which one was the best and this one was it. She had been going to the library to use the computer because she didn't want to rush out and purchase anything; she was investing in her future.

Mustafa grabbed her chin and kissed her deeply again; making her happy, made him happy. Just like last time, she didn't pull away. Just like last time, the bulge in his pants rose again.

Aunt Nellie interrupted them again. "Wasn't that nice of him Azure? King, you are such a sweet boy, I know Hattie Mae is proud of you."

They broke the kiss and both of them looked at Aunt Nellie. Azure knew if her aunt weren't there, she probably would be laid across the dining room table with her legs in the buck. Her pussy was throbbing; it felt like it had a life of its own.

"Let me help you clean up these dishes. I'm going to take Mustafa out for a drink to thank him for buying me the computer."

He took the hint and he started to help clear the table, as well. When they were in the kitchen, he stopped her before she went back into the dining room and pulled her close to him. "I want you so bad. Please spend the night with me."

"I will, but let's clean up this kitchen first." Azure got the last of the dishes and they washed, dried, and put the dishes up so fast. They headed out the door together hand in hand with Aunt Nellie standing there smiling.

Instead of taking her to his house or his condo, he got a suite in the Melia. He wanted to start ripping her clothes off on the elevator, but he remained calm. He wanted to pin her up against the elevator and kiss her into submission, but he didn't.

They got off on the top floor and he fumbled with the keycard opening the door. He couldn't hide his nervousness. He actually felt like this was his first time ever being with a woman. As soon as they got on the other side of the door, Azure surprised him and she was the aggressor. She was on him like a cheap suit. She was coming out of her clothes and kissing him passionately at the same time.

Mustafa was happy that her hands were steady enough to unbutton the buttons because that definitely was a no win situation for him.

"Wait a minute baby, let me calm my nerves or trust me I'm going to be no good for you. I need to blaze one right quick." He sat down in a lounge chair and pulled out a small sandwich bag filled with buds of weed that were vacuumed sealed separately. He looked around for something to cut open one of the vacuum packs with because it was so tight that he couldn't pry it open with his fingers.

Azure reached in purse and got out a small manicure kit and handed him a pair of small cuticle scissors. As soon as he sliced the package open, the pungent aroma filled the hotel room. She shook her head and said, "That is why it was sealed so tightly. I don't think that I ever smelled weed that strong in my life and I used to be a smoker."

She walked over and turned Pandora on the Smart television. The soothing sounds filled the hotel suite as she lowered the lights.

He rolled the blunt tightly and lit it with his Cartier lighter. He closed his eyes and inhaled the thick smoke and held it in his lungs before it blowing it out in perfect circles that filled the air. Mustafa looked up and Azure was watching him in her bra and panties. He couldn't tell what she was thinking. It looked like her eyes had turned a darker shade of blue and she was looking so sexy.

He stood up after taking another pull on the blunt and walked towards her. He held the smoke in and lowered his mouth to hers and blew the smoke in her mouth. She wrapped her arm around his neck and pulled him closer to her as she lifted her head and blew the smoke into the air in perfect circles. She then kissed him passionately, their tongues performing a seductive dance as they rotated around each other.

Azure started to unbutton his shirt as he kissed her neck and shoulders. His full lips were softer than cotton as they traced a trail from her neck to her breast. She guessed the weed had relaxed him because his hands were no longer shaking as he expertly unclasped her bra with one hand while the other palmed her ass cheek.

She let out a soft moan. It felt so good to have a man's hand on her naked skin. She had been on her best behavior with Mustafa since she met him despite the fact that she had met him after doing five years of hard time.

"I swear I been wanting you since the first night that I seen you in Luxurious. Now it has intensified to the point that I need you. These days without you have been torture. Tell me what I have to do to make you mines, then I won't have to feel like that anymore." He was staring down into her eyes and they were changing colors, mesmerizing him.

Although he was saying all the right things, this was not what she wanted to focus on right now. She just needed to finally have sex. She quieted him by putting her lips on his as she fumbled with his belt buckle.

Azure felt the weed in her system. She could barely hold her eyes open and her skin was tingling. She felt good. She unbuttoned his pants, pulled them down, and dropped to her knees. When she looked up, Mustafa's eyes were low and he was biting on his bottom lip.

She didn't expect it to be that big; she gulped hard. It wasn't even fully erect and it was bigger then Max's penis. She might have bit off more than she could chew.

Mustafa was so excited. He hoped that he didn't ejaculate prematurely because of the built up anticipation he had. Nothing could have prepared him for the feeling that took over him when Azure placed his penis in her warm, wet mouth.

He closed his eyes tightly and his toes curled in shoes. A moan escaped his lips and her mouth went up and down on his penis and one of her hands cupped his balls. She teased the head with her tongue and then deep throated it. He felt her tonsils collapsing on the head and it was driving him crazy.

She was definitely an expert as she did not gag one time, but he did notice her eyes start to water. Azure took all the extra saliva that had pooled in her mouth and spit it on his penis as she jacked him off with her small hands. She took his balls into her mouth one at a time and sucked on them softly while humming.

He could no longer remain quiet because she was driving him insane. This definitely was not the first blowjob that he had gotten, but it sure was the best. He felt his orgasm build up and he was not ready to erupt. Mustafa pulled her up off of her knees to a standing position. He pushed her hair from her face then bent down and kissed her so hard that it took her breath away.

Azure could tell that she had did good with the blow job because Mustafa looked like he was going to devour her as he slipped his shoes off and his pants from around his ankles. He pulled her panties off and picked her up and carried her over to the bed. She could see her phone lighting up on the nightstand.

She didn't care; she knew that Mustafa was about to fuck the shit out of her. She was happy that she had inhaled the weed, maybe it would help with the pain that his extra large penis was about to bring to her. She was thinking of positions that they could do it in where it would be less painful for her. After all, she had not been penetrated in five years.

All those thoughts went out the window when she felt his tongue softly lapping at her clitoris over and over. She hollered out loud. "Jeeeeeeeeesus," and hissed while biting on her bottom lip. It didn't take much for the first orgasm to hit her like a freight train.

Her juices were sweet to him as he continued to lick them up. He pushed one finger inside of her slowly. Mustafa had to keep reminding himself to be g ntle with her because after the fellatio she gave him, he vanted to ravage her.

Azure started to gyrate her hips on his f ce as he pumped his finger in and out of her. The nex thing he knew she let out a loud growl and she was sq irting on him. This was something he had never experie ice in all his years. He was ready to feel her warmth on h n. He got

84

in between her legs and looked down at her. She looked heavenly with her golden curls spread around her face like a halo. Her lips were open partially and her eyes were telling him to come and get her. He bent his head to kiss her while guiding his penis into her warmth.

Azure grimaced in slight pain, but tried her best to take it. It was feeling good and hurting at the same time. She hoped that once he got inside the pain would ease up. She shifted under him, opening her legs more to take him in. He was blessed indeed because he had length and width. He had filled her up and she didn't even think that half of his penis was inside of her.

Mustafa moved slowly and gently out of her while kissing her and staring her right in her eyes. She closed her eyes because she really wanted this to be just a fuck, but it was so much more and she didn't think that she was truly ready for that. He put one leg on his shoulder, then he eased in deeper and another orgasm swept over her.

He felt his orgasm build up as he held both of her legs up over his shoulders and pounded her softly as possible. Mustafa felt like this girl could do no wrong; she without a doubt had the best pussy and head game that he ever had in his life. He erupted with force, a loud growl filling the hotel suite.

For the next eight hours, they talked, laughed, watched pay-per-view movies, ordered room service and had amazing sex. Now as she lay pinned under him, she suddenly remembered her phone had been vibrating majority of the night, but she was in la-la land.

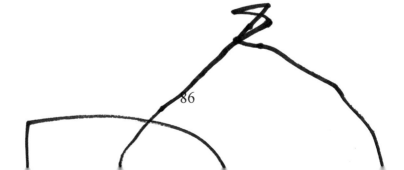

Chapter 12:

Aunt Nellie didn't ask any questions, she went right into the safe and got out fifty thousand dollars in cash, all one hundred dollar bills and gave them to her niece. She knew that Azure knew how to make money, and knew how to spend money wisely. She didn't have one worry as she turned over part of her life savings that she earned when she was out doing her thing in the streets. That was one of the reasons why she related to her so much because she remembered those days when a regular nine to five wasn't cutting it.

Her husband is what kept her grounded in her wild days. She was wild before him and she got wild again after he died. But then she remembered that she had to stop all that hot shit in the streets cause she was all Azure had. She woke up and realized that if she got banged up, who would take care of the little girl but the state.

Azure was walking slowly and she still felt a little pain in her midsection. Mustafa had definitely bought the pain. The pain and pleasure that she had experienced was way more than she expected. It seemed the more that she tried to put it out of her mind, the more she was having flashbacks of the entire day, even them sitting at the table eating the dinner Aunt Nellie had cooked. She knew about them nevers, so she wasn't going to say them, she was just going to try her damndest to not fall in love with this man, cause he definitely was the whole package, a big perfect package at that.

Her phone was vibrating again; she had just talked to Rocky less than an hour ago and told him that she was on the way with the money. He had it set up to get the majority of the work from Solo. She answered the phone slightly agitated. Azure didn't need Rocky knowing everything she had going on. She trusted him, but she had learned the hard way to never let anybody know your every move. "I'm on my way Rocky, I just met with Peebo to get the cash."

Before Aunt Nellie could say anything, Azure zipped up the blue Gucci purse that Fatt Mama bought her and held up her pistol to let her know that she was going to be safe before she left out the door to jump in her truck. Butterflies filled her stomach as she drove over to the spot on Hollywood Road. She was making the necessary steps to secure her future.

Rocky had furnished the place since the last time she had been over. It looked nice and clean. But the two amber colored Pyrex pots on the stove let you know that you were in a trap house. He had downgraded from a six-bedroom house to a condo, so he had a storage space full of nice furniture.

He'd rented a U-Haul truck and rounded up some junkies and went and loaded up. He planned on being there all the time running his sack back up so he needed it to be as comfortable as possible.

Azure walked in and looked around and she was impressed. A lot had changed in the last few days since she had been over; it was looking great. She gave Rocky a smile and a thumb up. "You did the damn thang with this bro. I like this." She sat down on the smoke grey leather sofa and opened her purse and took out the cash.

Rocky got crunk seeing the money. "That is what the fuck I'm talking bout right here sis. Lets turn this fifty thousand into some millions." He shook her hand and did the handshake that Max did with all his crew.

"Money Team 2014 baby, lets make this shit grow, so I can bring my better half home and open my boutique." Azure got up from the sofa just as quickly as she sat down. She was tired; after all, she had been up fucking all night.

Rocky placed the bundles of rubber-banded bills inside of a MCM backpack. "I didn't mean to keep calling you over and over again, I just didn't want dude to think I was bullshitting bout getting the work." He was ready to make the transaction; he already had some of his old customers lined up. The quicker he got off of his first pack, the quicker he could start to get the other shit he wanted to sell. He had already talked to D.J. from Hollywood Court about putting him on with the lean and he had the connect on the weed. His main focus was to make the money and reinvest it over and over. He followed Azure out the door and got in the corv te as she got in her truck.

Her phone buzzed as she went do n D. L. Hollowell Pkwy about to get on the highway to l. ad home and hibernate for the rest of the day. It was Mustafa. She remembered when this was the infamous Bankhead Highway, the home of Bankhead Courts and Bowen Homes Housing Project. Both sets of the projects were gone and so were a lot of the people, but it will always be Bankhead Highway to her.

"Hey baby, what are you doing?" Mustafa was in his pickup truck turning from Hollowell Pkwy to Harwell Road headed to the Blue Flame strip club to meet with one of his old school partners when he seen Azure speeding down the street. He wanted to see if she was going to tell the truth.

"Just getting on the expressway at Bankhead and 285. I'm still tired from last night, I'm bout to go home and soak my sore body and hibernate for a while." Azure got off at her exit and was anticipating her bed. She thought she might skip the hot bath and just immediately get in the bed.

"Well, I wish I could be in the bed with you, but I'm taking care of some business, I was just thinking about you and decided to call you." Mustafa was smiling ear to ear as he walked into the dark club; he knew he had him something special.

Chapter 13:

The presence of Aunt Nellie and Fatt Mama standing over her jarred Azure awake. She was shocked for a minute. She didn't know where she was, she actually had just been dreaming that she was in the same hotel that her and Mustafa had visited, but that this time she was with Max. The fact that this dirty bitch was the one who woke her from a dream about her King, made her jump up out the bed with a major attitude.

"Come on sleeping beauty, shake it off. We need your level head in this. Rocky was robbed and shot, he is in critical condition at Grady," Fatt Mama said, breathlessly.

Azure felt like she had just gotten sentenced to sixty more months in prison when she heard what Fatt Mama said. "Nooooooooooooooooooooooooooooooo!" she screamed as tears started to pour down her face. She was immediately filled with all kinds of emotions; shock, worry, frustration, doubt, panic, and then she started feeling physical pains in her head, heart, and stomach.

"Calm down baby girl, lets pray. Repeat after me. Heavenly Father we asked that you send a fleet of healing angels down to that hospital to protect Rocky. Let those angels touch the hands of everybody who come in contact with him from the patient transporters, to the doctors.

Heal him lord and make him better than befor . Amen."
Aunt Nellie grabbed her niece in a tight embrace and held
her tightly. She felt her shaking like a leaf on t e tree in
the fall. She hated to see her in pain. Rocky as like a
brother to her and he was the last tie that she ha to Max.

"Amen," Fatt Mama said as she looked at Aunt
Nellie and Azure enviously. Even without a drop of
makeup and that hideous scar down the side of her face
Azure was still breathtaking.

She tried to channel all of her positive thoughts
and energy because she really just wanted to ball up in a
knot and die. She had given Rocky the money that was the
beginning of her future. As always, it seemed like just
when total happiness was on the brink, it was snatched
away from her.

Azure went into the restroom and slipped on something
to go to the hospital. But before she exited the restroom,
she dropped to her knees to pray for her brother.

"Come on girl you can ride with me," Fatt Mama
said to Azure when she came out fully dressed.

"Nawl, I'm good, I preciate it, though." Azure
grabbed the Celine bag that Mustafa had bought her along
with the still sealed up box with her new computer in it
and headed out the door.

The look of contempt on Fatt Mama's face couldn't
be hidden; she was watching Azure's every move. Aunt

Nellie noticed her shooting daggers in the direction of Azure as the three of them headed toward the front door of the house.

She had seen this look on her face over the years when she would catch the two of them together. She knew that Fatt Mama was envious of her; she always has been, but now it seemed as if the older they got the more she noticed. The wheels started turning in her head as she watched them walk down the steps to their vehicles. Something wasn't right and she could feel it in her bones.

"I will call you after I find out everything and if my people come by, don't go running your mouth. Just tell him to call me." Azure blew her aunt a kiss before getting in her truck.

Fatt Mama watched this exchange before she got inside her car. She wondered who Azure's people were. Her cellphone started to ring and it was one of her workers calling her. She answered and found out that Solo was also shot today during the same robbery that Rocky was involved in earlier. She didn't even know that they hung out together. But she learned from the great Azure herself that get money niggas hung around other get money niggas.

■■

Azure sat inside of her truck inside of the parking deck of Grady hospital. She was filled with worry. She opened the box with the computer and smiled as she thought about how Mustafa was one surprise after another. She sure could use a hug from him right now. She wanted to hear those four magic words with some strong arms wrapped around her. "Everything will be alright".

She placed the laptop, manuals, and cords into the oversized Celine bag. Setting up the computer would give her something to do while she waited with Rocky. She didn't plan on leaving his side until he was showing some progress.

She didn't expect the emergency waiting room to be so crowded when she walked through. She threw on a sleeveless black cat suit and topped it with an oversized caramel cowl neck sweater and her knee high Minnetonka moccasins. She didn't ever run a comb through her bushy curls much less her fingers. She washed her face, brushed her teeth and didn't even care about how she looked to anyone. Rocky's health was her only concern.

She went to the admission's desk to find out where Rocky was and what was going on. She was surprised when his mother came from out of nowhere and hugged her.

"I thought that was you, but I didn't know. You look different, but in a good way. You look so beautiful Blue.

Rocky was just telling me the other day that you were home and that you were doing great. I told him that I was mad because you had not been to visit. You know you and Max were like my own. Did you get my cards, letters and packages baby?"

"Yes, ma'am I did. Thank you so much, I appreciate all of it including you keeping me in your prayers. I know it was the prayers and intercession of others that helped keep me whole in that hellhole. I hope you received my letters and cards, as well." Azure hugged Rocky's mom and followed her past security to the back.

The first person she seen when she walked through the double doors was Mustafa pacing back and forth with his telephone at his ear. He was barking out orders. He then looked up and seen her. His face lit up and his grimace turned into a smile. He ended the call and rushed over to her.

She really was his angel. She gave him a slight smile and threw herself into his outstretched arms.

Chapter 14:

Fatt Mama's mouth dropped when she seen King rush to Azure and pick her up in the air. Her breath literally left her body when she seen him kiss her deeply before putting her back on the floor. She automatically started to grind her teeth like she always did when she was mad. Not again.

She got up from the chair and went to the restroom because she felt that her frustration was going to start to show. As soon as she got around the corner, she stomped toward the restroom and pushed the door open with force.

Fatt Mama stood at the counter and looked at herself in the mirror. Her eyes started to water a little. She balled up her fist and hit the counter with enough force to break her hand. "Ahhhhhhhhhhh! Why do that bitch always win? Whyyyyyyyy?" she screamed at her reflection.

The tears steadily fell down her face. She felt like she was going to be always living in her shadow. It seemed like she could never get a one up on Azure. Everything was perfect until she got out of prison. She had lost weight, had plastic surgery, changed her image and she was now finally happy. Fatt Mama felt the only thing that was missing was the boss nigga at her side. But as long as Azure was in the picture, no one will ever feel as if she was good enough.

Just the thought of how she spent what seemed like her lifetime trying to measure up to Blue made her just want to ball up in a knot. But she didn't, because she knew that she couldn't show defeat. She would just have to come up with another way to cut her down. Fatt Mama grabbed a few paper towels from the dispenser and patted her face and her eyes trying not to mess up her make up.

She returned to the waiting room and found King and Azure sitting together on a chair. He had his arm around her and she was sitting in the chair leaning on him with a small computer in her lap as he explained something to her. He smiled at her and laughed at something that she said. Fatt Mama could see it, the same look that she remembered seeing in Max's eyes when he looked at Azure… Love.

Instead of sitting under them to hear what they were talking about, she sat across the room and pulled her phone out. Fatt Mama acted like she was texting someone as she secretly took pictures of King and Azure as they smiled, laughed, and cuddled with her smartphone. She was thankful for the camera on her Samsung Galaxy 5. Even though she was across the room the pictures came out crystal clear.

Fatt Mama smiled to herself when she imagined the backlash that was going to come from the pictures once Max got his hands on them.

Rocky's mom came into the waiting roo ı looking around. She could barely see Azure because she was dwarfed by King's large frame. "Baby girl, ı ıcky just woke up and you were the first person he asked ır."

Azure smiled, place the computer in King's lap and got up and followed behind Rocky's mom.

As soon as she was out of sight, Fatt Mama got up and moved closer to King, who continued to focus his attention on the laptop. Everything about him screamed powerful. She cleared her throat. "It's sad when a motherfucker ain't even safe in his own hood. I hope that the both of them come out of this A-1."

"Don't worry, they will and everybody who had something to do with what happened is going to die. You can bet your bottom dollar on that," King said through clenched teeth without even looking up. He couldn't wait until Solo woke up so he could tell him what happened.

Hearing King's response to her statement sent chills down her spine. Fatt Mama didn't even know that Solo would be the one that was serving Rocky. If she did she wouldn't have set the whole robbery up. She just wanted Rocky to pay for rejecting her and to stop Azure in her tracks now that she had came up with a plan to get back on top.

Chapter: 15

Rocky opened his eyes slowly when he felt her presence near. "I'm sorry lil' sis. I fucked up bad. Didn't I?"

Azure was just happy that he was alive. Anything could have happened. "No money in the world would've brought you back if you would have died. I wouldn't have been anymore good after that. I wouldn't have even been able to tell Max that you were gone."

"I tried to stop them. I wasn't gonna just let them take your money like that. How is Solo? I think he worse than me. He got shot in the back trying to run. He dropped the duffle bag. Who ever got us, they got the money and the work." Rocky's voice was low and raspy. He was still drugged up and in pain.

Her heart was saying one thing and mind was saying another. She said what was on her heart. Rocky was like her brother and he was just almost killed trying to help her achieve her dreams. "Don't worry about it. Just pray for Solo as well as yourself. Everything happens for a reason."

Azure leaned over the bed and kissed him on his forehead and walked back out into the hallway. Rocky closed his eyes. He had blown his chance to take back off. All his years in the streets and he had never been shot. He didn't know what went wrong. Those niggas had to have followed Solo to his spot because the only people that knew where he was now was Azure, Solo, and Fatt Mama. He shook the thought from his head. She wouldn't do that... or would she?

Rocky recalled their last conversation. She wasn't acting like she usually acted. Usually, she had a big attitude whenever he called her for some pussy. He had to admit, she was fine as hell now and she was getting her own money. But no matter how much folks called her Lil' Blue, she would always be Fatt Mama to him.

The same Fatt Mama that Max had warned him would be his downfall because she was nothing but a snake. He cut her off as soon as Max told him that, but he didn't stop fucking her. He couldn't, because everything was A-1. Fatt Mama let Rocky do everything to her in the bed. He stuck his dick in every hole in her body and he enjoyed it, too. That was why he couldn't stop fucking her all together because she was the best he ever had. But he kept her at an arm's length.

She got to his spot like within ten minutes after his call. He had just sealed the deal with Solo and now it was a go and he was just waiting for the money from Azure so that he could purchase the two bricks of pure cocaine. He was a ball of nerves. He was anxious as hell and after

100

drinking two shots of patron and smoking three blunts the anxiety didn't go away.

Rocky knew exactly what he needed—to catch a good ass nut. He also knew the only person who could do that was Fatt Mama. He debated on calling her because every since they broke up, her attitude was so damn nasty.

Rocky opened the door for Fatt Mama and she was dressed like she always was going to the club. Stilettos, tight jeans, blouse, Chanel bag, her hair and make up were flawless. She sauntered into the place like she owned the place and took a seat on the sofa.

"So, what do I owe this pleasure?" Fatt Mama asked as she crossed her legs tightly. Just the sight of Rocky had her pussy throbbing. It was like no matter when he called or how mad she was, she would go running.

"Trust me, the pleasure is mine always." He joined her on the sofa where he pulled her close to him and kissed her passionately. His hands roamed all over her breast in the sheer Versace shirt. "Take this off," he said as he pulled his shirt over his head.

Fatt Mama loved seeing him without his shirt. She started kissing on his tattoos on his chest and torso and running her hands up and down his muscular arms.

"I said take it off, in fact take all the damn clothes off," Rocky said as he unbuttoned his pants and took off his jeans and shoes. His dick was already rock hard. He couldn't wait until she put her mouth on it.

She stood up and stripped seductively. She loved him and hated that he didn't want her like she wanted him. It pissed her off. The only time she seen him was when he was out in public doing his thing or when he called her to fuck. Fatt Mama squatted in front of him between his legs and took his entire length into her mouth.

Rocky hated to admit that she was like his addiction. No matter what he did, she was the only thing that gave him that euphoric feeling. He watched her lick, suck, slobber, and devour his shaft. The ringing of his cellphone in the pocket on his jeans on the floor broke the silence. Well not really silence cause the moistness from Fatt Mama's mouth going to town on his dick filled the room.

Whoever it was, hung up and called again. The phone didn't stop ringing. Rocky stopped her because he remembered that he was supposed to be taking care of business. He was waiting on Azure to bring the money and he was waiting on some more people to call him about some money moves.

Fatt Mama looked up at him like he was crazy when he stopped her. She was into her groove. Saliva dripped from her mouth, because it seemed like he practically ripped his penis out of it. "Damn, what the hell is wrong with you?"

"I'm sorry shawty. I'm just in the process of making some money moves. That could be Azure, I'm waiting on her to come through to drop something off," Rocky said, nonchalantly.

She instantly became sick to her stomach. She decided to play it off. Fatt Mama smiled like everything was all good. Since she didn't have any contact with Azure, she could pick Rocky to see what she had going on.

"That's no problem. I barely get to see my cousin. Every time I go over Aunt Nellie's house she is never there. I guess she be with you, huh?"

"Nawl, she don't be with me like that. She be with her new nigga. Sis, is on some whole other shit now. But you know what ever she touches turns to gold. She just like cream, she always rises to the top," Rocky said smiling as returned Azure's call.

Fatt Mama thought to herself. "Not if I have anything to do with it." She listened to Rocky talking to Azure as she slipped her clothes back on. She knew she looked fly so she sat down on the sofa and crossed her legs. The Medusa head on her Versace heels was gleaming just like her jewelry.

"I will just hit you up when she leaves. Maybe you can come back through if you aren't busy." Rocky stood at the door holding it open.

She couldn't believe that he was putting her out. He was putting her out for Azure. She was pretty sure that the shock registered on her face even though she remained silent. Her feelings were hurt. "I'm pretty sure that I will be busy." She brushed past him as she walked out the door.

Rocky grabbed her arm. "This is bout some money. I'm bout to be back on top soon."

She got in her car as the wheels turned in her head. She had to figure out what Rocky and Azure was up to. Fatt Mama knew for a fact that if Azure had anything to do with it, it had a great return.

As she jumped on the highway, she turned up her radio and Future's new smash hit 'Move dat dope' blared through her speakers. Then it hit her, Azure had come up with some money and Rocky was about to flip it.

But where in the world did she get that type of money? Maybe she had it put up. Or maybe it came from whomever the new nigga was she was fucking with. Fatt Mama knew for a fact that the Nigerians had not given her any money. She was fucking with one of them and to her knowledge; Azure had not had any contact with them since she'd been home.

The conversation with Azure on the day she took her shopping replayed in her head. One thing about the truth, it usually always hurt. She was tired of getting her feelings hurt and it always came back to Azure. She was going to put a stop to that. "Call Bandit," Fatt Mama said to her Bluetooth. The phone rung three times and then a male with a raspy voice picked up.

"Blue, what it do, Ma?" His New York accent was heavy. He always reminded her of DMX when he talked.

"Got a fool lick for you. It's gonna be like taking candy from a baby," she said as she gave him the details and told him to bring her the money and he could keep the work.

Chapter: 16

Azure came back out to the waiting room and King was deep in conversation on his cellphone. He didn't look up as he growled directions into the phone. She could tell that he was beyond angry about his friend getting shot. After what Rocky told her what happened, she silently said a prayer for Solo as she walked back to the waiting room. She didn't know him personally, but on the one occasion that they were in each other's presence he was a really nice guy with a cool, laid back demeanor.

She was surprised that none of his family and friends had showed up yet, because the other waiting room was filled with Rocky's loved ones. The word had hit the Westside and everybody was coming down to the hospital. Security had to clear them out of the front waiting room where they were and put them in the one in the back. Azure snuggled into King's side as he talked on his phone. She closed her eyes, but then she suddenly opened them fast as she felt someone watching h r.

Fatt Mama's stomach was doing somer ults. She didn't know if it was from the nervousness of hat King had said earlier or if it was because of her built p hatred for Azure. She looked at them with disgust. She just couldn't put her hand on it. What in the hell di she have that always drew these guys to her? What was she saying to them? Fatt Mama wasn't worried about the sex department because she knew she was a beast. She turned up on ten on whomever she was with. It was just she never attracted the main man.

King ended his phone call and put his arm around Azure and pulled her close. He was so happy that she was here with him. He was an only child; Solo was the closest thing that he had to a brother. But he was curious how she knew what was going on? He had seen her leave with an older woman. He didn't like any surprises especially where he was involved.

"Bae, what is going on? I was so happy to see you that I didn't even ask you how you knew that I was here." King stretched his long legs out. He felt someone watching them. He looked up and Fatt Mama was staring at them without blinking. He felt uncomfortable under her glare. He stood up and pulled Azure up with him.

"Where are we going?" she asked as she took the laptop from him and placed it back into her Celine bag.

"For a walk, I need to stretch my legs," He said loud enough for all the ears around him to hear.

Azure spotted Fatt Mama when she held her head down like she had not been eyeballing them the entire time. "Okay, that is fine. I need a bottle of water anyway."

107

"If I hear anything about Rocky cuz, I will come and find you," Fatt Mama said to Azure's back as she exited the waiting room.

"Something ain't right about her. That is why I had to get up out of there." King had Azure's hand in his as they got on the elevator to head to the gift shop.

A chill went down her spine. It was crazy, because those were Max's first words when he met Fatt Mama for the first time. "You don't have to tell me. I learned it the hard way. They say keep your enemies close, but fuck all that. I don't want that bitch around me."

"Wait a minute? That is your cousin? I've seen her around before, hanging out with Solo." King was beyond confused now.

"Okay, here is what is going on. Your friend was meeting up with Rocky, who is like a brother to me. They both were robbed and shot. I was at home sleep, because as you know, I was dog as tired from being with you. Fatt Mama, or you might know her as Lil' Blue came over and woke me up and told me what happened and I rushed down here. I didn't know that anyone else had been shot with Rocky until I got down here." Azure went over the words in her head to make sure she had everything covered.

"Oh okay, that makes sense now. I emember Rocky was who you were coming to see the first light that

I met you at Luxurious." Now things were making a little sense to him.

"And that bitch ain't my cousin, she is just a stray that my aunt took in. We are not blood. I have not fucked with her since I been home. I do not have to get burned more than one time. She left me for dead literally when I was locked up. I'm not mad at that because nothing but some good came from it. If I wouldn't have went through that struggle I wouldn't be the strong woman standing before you today."

As the walked into the gift shop, they bumped into Rocky's mom coming out. She placed her hand on King's arm. "Your brother is in my prayers."

A smiled spread across his face as he looked down at her. He could feel her genuine spirit radiating from her. "Thank you, Ma'am. Your son is in mines, as well. The both of them are going to walk out of here better than ever. Grady is one of the best trauma hospitals in the country. These doctors are going to get them right.

"You showl is right about that there baby. There is no other place that I rather he would be and I got the bumper sticker on my car to prove it," she said, as she laughed likely.

"We will be right back up there in a few minutes and I will come over to the waiting room, so I can see the family," Azure said to Rocky's mom. She had grown really close to his entire family in the years that they had been friends.

"I need to hurry back up there. I hope that damn Fatt Mama haven't snuck in the back and upset my baby. That girl is a real pain in the ass. I was so happy when he broke up with her. If I hear one peep out of her, I'm getting security to escort her ass right on out the front door." She turned and rushed toward the elevators.

Azure stood still. She was trying to process what Rocky's mother had just said to her. Fatt Mama must've started fucking with Rocky after her and Ma went to prison. Funny thing is, neither one of them ever mentioned it to her. She was going to let Rocky get some rest, but she was going to grill his ass as soon as he woke up. She also had a bone to pick with Aunt Nelli, because she knew that she knew something was going on

Chapter: 17

Fatt Mama sat in the waiting room alone in her thoughts. She was trying to see where she had gone wrong. She swore that once Azure went to prison that everything was going to be okay for her. But things didn't always go as planned. She had been feeding them information in hopes that they would get Azure. Little did she know they already had started building a case against Max.

When she found that out, she racked her brain trying to figure out how she could warn him, but still let Azure take the fall. Fatt Mama was trying to do four things; get Azure put behind bars, not implicate Max, not get their connect in trouble, and stay free her damn self so she could enjoy the fruits of her hard work. It became obvious that she didn't think things out as well as she should have on the first night that they were locked up.

The federal agent who she had been talking to told her that Max had taken the bulk of the charges that Azure was up against, as well. That fucked Fatt Mama up because she was hoping that Azure would take the bulk of the charges since she had never been locked up and Max would do little to no time and be free.

Fatt Mama had her eyes set on Max from the beginning. She figured that maybe him being behind bars and vulnerable might work to her advantage. She had tried to bond with Max, but he was not hearing that. She was mad at first, but she soon got over it. She had planned on helping to get him released and everything. But things didn't go as planned.

Max was big on loyalty. So he would never be with her. Fatt Mama used that to her advantage because she made it appear that Azure was disloyal. She started keeping her letters from him. And when he called to check on her, Fatt Mama would tell him that Azure called, but she didn't ask about him.

As she excommunicated Max and Azure, Fatt Mama realized that it might just be better to get with Rocky. He was free and he was the boss now.

Her money was coming in right. She picked up where Azure left off. She had taught her everything that she knew and she had recently introduced her to the connect, so it was only right that she took over. Fatt Mama knew that money attracted money, so that was when she started to transform herself.

First it was her hair and wardrobe, and then it was her surroundings. She started to go where she knew the bosses hung out at. Fatt Mama was mad because she still was not getting the attention that she had expected. She had bought all the fashion magazines that she had seen Azure buying and looking at all the time. She started to go to the boutiques and stores that she heard her talking about.

A lot of the stores did not sell clothing in her size. So that was when she went to a doctor who specialized in weight loss. The weight started to fall off quickly after she started taking the prescription weight loss pills. Her self-esteem started to rise, as the numbers on the scale got smaller.

Fatt Mama was leaving from getting her hair done in a long sew-in with the expensive hair that Azure always wore, she stopped by Rocky's spot. She hoped he saw the difference in her.

She was happy that there was only one car out front. She exhaled loudly as she knocked on the front door. She bit her bottom lip and twirled one of the tendrils on her finger nervously as she waited for someone to come to the door.

Rocky answered the door with a towel around his waist and a blunt in between his lips. He opened the door and seen that it was Fatt Mama. He turned around and walked and picked up the lighter off the counter and lit the blunt before he said something to her. He took a pull and blew perfect circles in various sizes in the air. He leaned against the wall wondering what did she want. There really wasn't a reason for her to be coming around now that Blue and Max were both locked up. He never really felt Fatt Mama anyway. It was just something about her that wasn't right and he never was able to put his finger on it.

Fatt Mama mouth watered at the sight of Rocky standing there in front of her. His caramel skin was still glistening with droplets of water. He walked toward her to hand her the blunt. She swallowed hard as he stood in front of her, looking down at her handing her the blunt. "There is something else I want to put my mouth on." She ripped the towel from his waist and scooted closer to the edge of the sofa as she put his limp dick in her mouth.

"Girl wait a minute. What in the hell are you doing? Don't do that? I got shit to do now." Rocky said loudly trying to get her to stop before she started.

If Fatt Mama didn't know how to do anything else she knew how to suck a dick. She had been sucking her thumb all her life. Rocky tasted as good as he looked. Her mouth got wetter as she clamped down on his throbbing penis tighter.

The fact that he didn't want the head at first didn't stop it from being some of the best that he ever had. So instead of protesting, he stood in the middle of the floor in the trap living room as Fatt Mama dropped to her knees off the sofa and gave him some monster dome.

She knew that he was into it now because she heard him moaning as he pumped his hips forward as she sucked, licked and slobbered on his penis that had doubled in size. Her pussy was getting super wet from his reaction to the blowjob. She could see his toes curling and uncurling on the carpet as he tried to stay standing up straight as she sucked his dick like it was the last dick that she would ever suck.

"Wait a minute, dis shit too good. Let me sit down, my knees are about to buckle. He pulled his dick out her mouth and sat down butt naked on the sofa. Fatt Mama stood up and pulled off the Nike shorts that she had on and kicked off her Airmax and crouched down in between his legs.

Her pussy was gushing wet as she put her hand in between her legs and started to masturbate as she continued sucking Rocky's dick. All you could hear in the room was the moaning from the both of them and the wetness coming from her mouth and her pussy. She worked her swollen clitoris in a circular motion as her head bobbed up and down in his lap.

Fatt Mama held her head up and took a deep breath as the orgasm hit her. She bit down on her bottom lip hard as her eyes rolled in the back of her head. Her pussy was throbbing so bad and she wanted to feel him inside of her. "Can I feel you? I need to feel you." She panted looking him in the eyes as he jacked his dick while she had been taking care of herself.

"Put your fingers in your mouth. Let me see you suck your juices off your fingers." Rocky couldn't deny that Fatt Mama had the wettest mouth that he had ever been inside of. The slobbering sounds were driving him crazy. He pulled her fingers out of her mouth and put his dick back in it. He wasn't really trying to fuck her. Dick tend to drive hoes crazy.

Her pussy was contracting and throbbing hard, but he act like he didn't want to give her the dick. Fatt Mama thought to herself that she was going to have to go full throttle. That was the thing about her, she rarely had sex cause she always seemed to fall in love, but when she did, she fucked like a porn star.

She surprised him and grabbed his legs and forced them into the air. She then proceeded to suck his balls softly one by one, while humming on them. Lathering them with her saliva, she alternated back and forth. Fatt Mama watched as Rocky reached down and started to jack his dick. It was rock hard and standing at attention.

"Oww shit! Bitch, what you trying to do to me? Damnit, that's it. Suck my motherfucking balls bitch. Your mouth so god damn wet. Don't stop," Rocky said as he stroked himself.

Fatt Mama knew that she had him just \ here she wanted him. She stopped licking his balls a d moved underneath. She looked up to see how he respor ed cause some niggas didn't play bout anything that close to their asshole. He closed his eyes and started panting as he stroked himself faster. He liked what she was doing to him; this was her cue.

She started to massage his balls softly while he stroked himself. Rocky's moaning had her about to cream without even being touched. Fatt Mama snaked her tongue out of her mouth and started to lick Rocky's asshole. After he didn't stop her after the first lick, she proceeded to lick and suck his asshole, as he moaned loudly and hissed.

He didn't know who taught her how to do what she was doing, but she was definitely an expert. He never had anyone to even try to do that to him. The shit was driving him crazy. His dick felt like it was about to bust. He reached down and pressed her face to his ass as she stuck her tongue in his asshole. It was like he was having an out of body experience. He was looking at himself moaning and groaning like a girl as he grinded on her face. His subconscious was telling him that a man should not be enjoying this so much, but his body was telling him to enjoy it.

Fatt Mama seen that she had Rocky right where she wanted him. His reaction to her caused her to go over the edge. She started to orgasm. She licked harder as she stuck two fingers inside of her dripping wet pussy.

"Oh shit! Oh shit! I'm bout to come," Rocky said louder than he wanted to.

Fatt Mama took his penis into her mouth sucked on it hard and started back to massage his balls as the warm sticky liquid shot down her throat. The loud roar that emerged from Rocky scared her. He shook one last time and collapsed back onto the sofa.

He covered his face and shook his head. He had never, ever had an orgasm like that in his life. He looked down at her and she was sitting on the floor in Indian style at his feet watching him. She had lost some weight and she was no longer wearing braids now. It was long and parted down the middle, it reminded him of how Blue used to wear her hair. "Brang yo' mother fucking ass over here right now. I know that pussy is ready for me to dig into."

Fatt Mama remembered Rocky fucking her every way but the wrong way. They fucked over all the trap house and it was just their luck no one came by because he was out of work. After that she was with him every day and she thought she was finally happy. Her weight continued to drop off and she was dressing like in the magazines. Rocky was taking her out of on the town; she was his girl.

Then one day everything changed. She had just come from the mall shopping for the Lil Wayne concert for the both of them when she stopped at the trap house to leave his clothes with him.

When she was let into the house by one of his workers, Rocky was standing at the stove. She already knew what he was doing even though he had his back to her. She could see the movement of his arm and tell that he was, "Water Whipping". The sound of the fork hitting the amber colored Pyrex boiler was all that could be heard. Fatt Mama put the bags down on the floor and went to give him a kiss. When he turned around he had a scowl on his face.

Instantly, she replayed whom she might have seen in the mall or who she had talked to today because she knew that she hadn't did anything personally to Rocky. "What's wrong, Bae?"

"I'm going to ask you two questions. I don't need an explanation, just strictly yes and no answers. Did you ever try to fuck with my brother? Did you have anything to do with them getting banged up?" He had just gotten off the phone with Max and he finally told him about his relationship with Fatt Mama.

Max had told him that Fatt Mama acted like she had the key to the jail and that if he fucked with her that she could get him out with no problem. He told Rocky that the only way she could have the key to get him out was if she had a hand in putting him in there.

Fatt Mama was taken aback by the questions. There was nothing like a sober mind and some time away from everyone to put shit in perspective. Max had been behind them bars playing connect the dots. She didn't say anything at first. She just stood there like a mute.

"So, you don't hear me or the fact that you aren't saying anything is an admission of guilt? Whatever it may be, I'mma need for you to get out of my face before I throw this hot dope on your slimy ass." Rocky was in shock. He actually thought that he was building something with Fatt Mama, that was one of the reasons that he waited to tell Max about them. He wanted to make sure that he had something solid first.

Fatt Mama never admitted to anything. She left the trap house in tears. She didn't even go to the concert. She sat in her condo and plotted in silence as she decided how she was going to pay Rocky for breaking up with her.

They never did get back together, but they did continue to fuck off and on. She didn't want to get back with him. She was now on top and he was scraping the bottom of the barrel. He never did bounce back after sh sent her people at him.

Some people never learn that its some folk you just don't fuck over and Fatt Mama just happened to be one of them. She got up from her seat in the waiting oom and headed to the closest drug store, so she could print the photos out and send them to Max.

Chapter: 18

After the shooting, Azure was walking around like a zombie. She was in shock. The fifty thousand dollars that they took was the seed money for her future. She really didn't want to take another risk and try to start over, but she didn't have any choice. She still had the same goals; open her boutique and bring Max home. Azure tried to rack her brain to come up with another way to get money and get it fast and nothing had a faster return than the dope game.

She thought that her Aunt was going to be extremely upset about the money; if she was she didn't show it. She still had her back and told her if she needed anything that she would help her. Azure didn't know where her little lady was getting these large sums of money from, but she definitely didn't seem to have a problem giving them to her.

Azure went to Peebo this time to get the money. He was happy to see her. He had wanted to reach out to her since she had been released. He put money on her account steadily while she was incarcerated. But he wanted to give her something to show his appreciation to her for not folding. He knew for a fact that if she had given him up to the authorities that she probably wouldn't have served one day behind bars.

She hadn't been getting much sleep lately and the dark circles around her eyes showed it. Twenty-four hours were definitely not enough hours in the day for her. It seemed like King had to see her everyday, but she was limiting her time with him.

Azure couldn't deny that she had started to develop feelings for him, but she was fighting with all her might not to fall in love and he was making it hard. She tried to devote as much time to her future and King was not in it.

Azure walked into Ocean Prime with her head held high despite the fact that her spirits were low. She was lead to the table where Peebo was already seated with his brother Toby.

She could see the shock register on his face when he stood up to hug her. He was surprised by her transformation.

Her face registered shock, as well, when he started speaking his Nigerian accent had disappeared. She remembered when she first met him; she used to have to strain herself to understand what he was saying because his accent was so thick.

"We are so happy that you are home. I was hoping I would have heard from you much sooner," Peebo said to Azure.

Azure had always been full of pride and she hated asking anybody for anything. She wasn't someone who usually had a sense of entitlement, but something had to be said about her not implicating them as the head of the organization. She had made these guys millions of dollars and she just hoped that they would help her get her business started. If she could just get her hands on another fifty stacks.

She had already been in touch with a new lawyer. She found out from Rocky that Max's former lawyer was locked up for embezzlement. She knew she needed to have at least ten thousand dollars in hand when she went to secure a new lawyer for him. She had been researching his case and it had more holes in it than Swiss cheese. This made her very optimistic that it was indeed a good chance on him coming home.

She had the Who and the What; she just needed the how. Hopefully, this was the how seated across the table from her. Azure listened as they caught her up on everything that had been going on while she was gone. They told her how they had reached out to Fatt Mama to pay for her a lawyer and was told that it was already taken care of. She shifted in her seat as her face turned beet red. Every time she turned around, she was hearing this bitch name attached to some negative shit. Max's words played over and over in her head.

She blanked out as they went on and on about things that had occurred with Fatt Mama while she was gone. She wanted to choke her with her bare hands. They told her that, they were only giving her light work b cause she had fucked up three big jobs.

Peebo offered to relocate Azure to Baltimore where she could have her own organization. They wanted her back. The offer was very tempting, but Azure didn't want to get back in the game.

"That offer sounds good, but those were the worst five years of my life. I just want to open up my business and bring my man home, so I can pick right back up when I left off," she told Peebo, trying to let him down as gently as possible. Azure didn't want to mess with no more paperwork. She knew the feds were looking for her to get right back into it.

Peebo's brother spoke up; his accent was still very heavy. "We understand. We appreciate all the hard work that you put in for us and if there is anything that we can do we will. But we really want you to think about this opportunity. We do not need an answer right now."

"Well, that is what I asked to meet with you guys. I'm turning over a new leaf and I need funds to do it. I want to know if you could reward me for my years of service and loyalty. Whatever you give me will be going to a good cause." Butterflies filled Azure's stomach when she finished asking them for the money. She didn't want to give an exact dollar amount because she didn't want to seem greedy.

He smiled and took his wallet out of his blazer pocket. Peebo took a pen and wrote her a check. He showed the amount to his brother who nodded his approval. He tore the check out of the book and handed it to Azure. He hoped that she would be able to do something with it.

Azure's hand shook slightly when she reached across the table to get the check from Peebo. Her blue eyes doubled in size when she seen that the check was for one hundred thousand dollars. She never imagined that they would have given her that much. She jumped up from her chair and gave both of the guys hugs. She didn't even want dinner. She wanted to go home as soon as possible and just jump up and down on her bed. "Thank you so much, you just don't know what this means to me."

Chapter: 15

Aunt Nellie walked down the hall to wake Azure up. Hattie Mae had just called and woke her up and gave her some bad news. King's friend Solo didn't make it. Three weeks had passed since the robbery and shooting that he was involved in. She felt so sorry for King. Hattie told her that he was like a brother to him and that he didn't have any family.

She knew that her niece had started to develop feelings for the young man. Nellie saw her running from the love that he was trying to give her. But that was the thing about love; you couldn't out run it. It would sneak up on you like a thief in the night and when you least expected it, you would be wallowing all in it. She saw how he looked at her, how he talked to her, how he showered her with gifts.

Aunt Nellie tapped on the bedroom lightly and twisted the doorknob and walked in. She jarred her lightly. Azure jumped up, her eyes buck.

"What's wrong auntie?" She knew it had to be something wrong if she was waking her up. Azure had just gotten home less than three hours ago, because she was with Rocky at his spot. They had been plotting and planning. Since she had gotten the money from Peebo, everything was going forward with vigor. She had paid for Max's lawyer, gave her aunt half of her money back, set aside fifty thousand for Rocky to get some work and put the rest into money market accounts.

"I've got some bad news baby. Hattie Mae just called. Solo has passed away. I think that you should go and be with King. He is going to need you right now."

Azure took a deep breath and bit her bottom lip to fight back the tears. She knew that King was in a lot of pain right now. He had just recently told her that Solo really had no one but him. He would have been perfect for Fatt Mama if she had taken the time to see the bigger picture. But her dirty ass didn't deserve a good nigga. Based on what her and Rocky had been talking about since he had been home, more than likely she was the reason that Solo was dead.

Rocky told Azure about how him and Fatt Mama hooked up when she was gone. How she went through her transformation period and got the big head. He told her about what Max said about her and how he broke up with her, and then he was robbed shortly afterwards. Rocky couldn't deny the fact that he was addicted to the sex and that was what kept him close to her in some shape, form, or fashion.

There was no way around the fact that Fatt Mama was a big problem that needed to be stopped. She couldn't believe that she was that dirty. Azure came home and laid in the bed thinking about all the trouble that had been around her that probably could be traced back to Fatt Mama.

Her plan was to get the discovery packet for her case as soon as possible, because it was something in her spirit telling her that Fatt Mama had something to do with her and Max getting banged up in the first place.

"Damnit, that is messed up. I do need to go and be with him. Auntie I don't want to love this man. I can't love this man. Max is about to come home soon," Azure said as she got out of the bed to head to her bathroom to shower.

Aunt Nellie followed behind her and stood in the bathroom door. "Have you ever thought that you were sent this man so you could see how powerful love is? This man is fighting to be with you. You don't think you deserve someone to fight for you? You are running from him, and he continues to catch up with you. You attempt to not call him, and he don't call you; he shows up. You won't go out to eat with him because you say you are busy; he brings the restaurant to you. You won't go shopping with him; he brings you everything the store has in your size. You won't talk to him; he sits under you in silence. That is fighting. I haven't seen Max send you a letter since you been home. I haven't heard you saying that you even got a call from him, but I do know that you just dropped ten thousand dollars to get him a lawyer. You deserve to be someone who will fight for you baby. You are worth it, don't you ever forget that."

She was fighting back the tears, but when she got in the shower she let them fall. Azure refused to give up on Max. She was trying her best to show him that she had his back, but Aunt Nellie was right he didn't seem to care about her anymore.

Rocky had not said anything about him calling saying thanks for the lawyer. She was sure that he knew that he had new counsel that she had paid for. Maybe he felt like that was what she was supposed to do since he took the majority of her time for her.

Azure just wanted what she thought what her life was supposed to be like. She wanted her dreams to come true. Her dreams were of her and Max being married with children and to have successful businesses. Her shoulders fell forward in defeat, just because she wanted it, maybe that was not what the creator had intended for her.

She dried off and got out the shower. She dressed in haste throwing on some camouflage pants, and a denim shirt with a pair of Giuseppe sneakers that King had bought her. She left out the house with a lot on her mind and rushed to be with him.

Chapter 15:

Fatt Mama sat outside of Solo's condo with tears in her eyes. She did not mean for him to get hurt, now he was dead because of her. She had not been able to sleep, so she wanted to go to the hospital to sit with him while no one was there. She had so much built up inside of her and she thought that if she could just apologize for causing all of this everything would be alright.

When she arrived to his floor, she went straight to his hospital room and when she walked inside housekeeping was inside of the room stripping the bed of its linen. "Excuse me, do you know where they have transferred him to?"

"He passed on about two hours ago ma'am," the older black lady said as she started to spray down the bed with disinfectant.

Fatt Lady was frozen in one spot as the tears fell from her eyes. She was in shock. She couldn't believe he was gone. He was a good nigga, he just got caught in the crossfire of some bullshit that he didn't have anything to do with it. Her heart was heavy. There had to be some way she could get some peace from the situation. Maybe if she helped his family pay for his funeral service, her emotional load might be lightened. She decided to head to his house, so that she could talk to his family.

She expected more people to be there. Maybe they had not heard about it yet. There was only a Range Rover and Azure's Mercedes truck parked out front. Fatt Mama let out a loud sigh as she checked her face in the mirror to make sure that her makeup was still in check. It was like no matter how she started the race Azure always got to the finish line before her.

Fatt Mama got out the car and headed to the front door. As she approached, she heard a male's voice talking in a very loud manner. She could tell that they were upset. Instead of pushing the doorbell, she stood and listened to what was being said.

"I got the money to put a price on the head of everybody that had something to do with this. But trust me when I find out who is responsible for the death of my brother, I'm going to kill them. I got to. I know that is the only way I'm going to be able to sleep. All he ever wanted was to make some money and have a family. All these slime ass niggas out here in the game, why did he have to be the one to die?" King was pacing back and forth in the living room.

Azure watched him and she hurt for him. She had been thinking on her way over to the house how could she tell him that she knew who had something to do with it. As she watched his reaction, she wondered did Fatt Mama really deserve to die at the hands of King. She was like family to her, but then Solo was like family to King. He didn't do anything wrong and Fatt Mama did everything wrong.

"Now, I gotta put this man in the ground. He didn't have anybody but me. My grandmother is heartbroken. She looked at Solo like he was her blood. She is too old to be dealing with this type of shit. This ain't right and that is why somebody got to pay and pay quickly. I got one hundred thousand dollars to the first person who can bring me his shooter."

Fatt Mama panicked as she finally pressed the doorbell. Part of her wanted to turn around and walk away, but she had to see who else was on the other side of the door. She needed to see who she might be up against. Then she thought to herself, no one knew of her involvement except her people who she had put on the lick.

Azure sat and thought to herself that the m ney King was offering would be more than enough for Rocky to get back right. She had to talk to him immediately. Maybe he could try to remember everything, come up with something that will point them in the direction of the perpetrators, because it was obvious that Fatt Mama was not the shooter. She was just the mastermind behind it.

She got up and went to answer the door, she was sure that the word was out now and that friends were going to start pouring in to pay their respects. Azure couldn't make out who the female was on the other side of the door because of how the stain glass was patterned. She opened the door and when she saw that it was Fatt Mama, she wanted to slam the door in her face.

"Man, your balls are bigger than I imagined. You really got some nerve coming here."

"I just wanted to come and pay my respects to his family and offer whatever assistance I could in paying for his funeral services. Just because I didn't date him, he was still a friend," Fatt Mama said as she pushed past Azure. She walked into the place like she owned it and approached King. She held her arms open to give him a hug.

Azure stood off to the side with her nose tooted up and her eyebrow in the air as she watched the performance that Fatt Mama was putting on. She heaved a sigh. She wanted to knock her head off of her shoulders.

"I'm so sorry for your loss. Solo was a good guy. If only we had met in another day and time. I woke up with him on my mind and went to the hospital to sit with him and when I got there they told me that he had passed," Fatt Mama said as she stood close to King after their embrace. She gave Azure the side eye.

"I appreciate your condolences. I remember seeing you two together. What is your name again?" King said trying to place the young lady who stood in front of him dressed like she was about to go to the club. What stood out most about her was the blue contact lenses that contrasts so much with her dark skin.

"You might have heard him talk about me, we did date. He called me Blue," Fatt Mama said, proudly.

King couldn't hide his reaction when she said her name. He did remember Solo mentioning her; he really liked her. He bragged about how she was on her own get money shit and that she wasn't a gold digger. He just couldn't get her to get with his campaign, though. He looked at Azure and he noticed the familiarity in her eyes.

"Yeah, everybody calls you Blue now, but there will always only be one real Blue. Ain't that right Fatt Mama? My auntie always said that imitation was the greatest form of flattery. But the funny thing about this is that it makes me sick to my stomach way more than it flatters me. But you know what they say, everybody gotta have a dream." Azure was tired of the whole Hakuna matata vibe. She was tired of holding all this shit in.

"I see that I might have came at the wrong time. I just wanted to offer my condolences. He was a special person and I also wanted to offer any financial help that I could. I know that a lot of people in our community don't have life insurance." Fatt Mama tried to keep her facial expression as blank as possible, but it was hard cause she wanted to frown. Her hate for Azure grew by the minute.

"I appreciate your offer lil' mama. I'm trying hard not to take it as an insult. I was raised by my grandmother and we don't hold no damn fish fries when our people die. We have insurance policies, not to mention I'm one of the richest men in the city. We don't need your help trust me.

134

Do like everybody else and send a flower," King said looking at her with the look of disgust on his face.

Chapter 15:

"I'm trying to think lil' sis. Everything happened so fast. I sure hate that he died. He was a real stand up guy, that is one of the reasons why I chose to do business with him. You know that I really don't trust easily," Rocky said to Azure, who had just came over to visit him at the spot. He had just got a shipment of promethazine in. He was still sore because one of the bullets were still inside of him. It was lodged between his ribs. But he had to get to work. He had promised Azure that he was going to pay her back the money that was taken during the robbery.

"That one hundred thousand will put ou right where you need to be. I'm not trying to put ʒ ʌu off on King; he has yet to reveal to me that Solo worke for him. I keep going with the guise that he gets all his m ney from his legitimate business holdings. But you know hat he is in the game." Azure still wanted to get some do ɛ, so that she could multiply her money quick, fast, and i a hurry. Everything was in motion; she wanted to be si ing on a nice chunk of change by the time that Max was leased.

"I know it will. I have had my ear to he street trying to see if any of the people I deal with had come across anything. You know the streets talk. I want the person's head who tried to take my life," Rocky said angrily.

"Well it's time for you to come out of denial. I sat there and listened to everything you told me when we were catching up when you were in the hospital and you already know who I think had something to do with everything. I hate to seem petty, because that is how people sound who always blame someone for their downfall. My gut is always right. I know Fatt Mama had something to do with us getting banged up and based on what you said; she had something to do with both of your robberies. You can be a fool if you want to and try to ignore it. I'm not. I just got the discovery packet in the mail from my case. I'm going through it with a fine tooth comb," Azure said as she patted her purse.

"What are you going to do if you find out that she did have something to do with y'all getting locked up? You aren't no killer, Azure?" Rocky said as he pulled his ringing phone out of back pocket.

"No, I'm not, but the two men that are in love with me are and the both of them have a far reach. What she has been doing has affected both of them. I can have a line around the building of motherfuckers who will do something to her with nothing but two words.... Get her."

Rocky half listened to Azure as he pressed five on his phone to accept the call from Max. He held up his finger to his mouth to let her know to be quiet. He put the phone on speaker. "Hey bro, what's good?"

"Boy, I'm so happy to hear your voice. You know that I have been in here going crazy. When I got word

137

through the pipeline that you had been shot in   robbery, I wanted to break out this muthafucker. How yc doing?" Max said excitingly, happy to hear his best friend's voice.

"Momma told me that she told you that I was recovering. She would have told you if I was in bad shape."

"Yeah, she would have, but then again I thought she was downplaying it, because she didn't want me to be worried about you in here. The new lawyer that Ol' girl sent came through. She is talking some good shit, but I'm not going to get my hopes up. I'm so tired of getting disappointed."

"I feel you bro, but Azure is working hard on your behalf out here on the outside. All that she talks about is bringing you home," Rocky said as he smiled at Azure sitting across from him.

"So you call fucking with the next big thing so that she can get money for a lawyer working on my behalf? What is she going to do if this shit that the lawyer is cooking up actually works. She is running around town everywhere with that nigga King. They look like they in love, all hugged up everywhere. Man shawty ain't bout to get me killed. I pray everything work out with the lawyer and the appeal. I'm being optimistic. So, I'm not going to say if I come home, but more like when I come home, I ain't fucking with shawty like that. She has changed and she just doing this cause she got a guilty conscience. I saw the pictures of her with her new nigga. I'm going to let

138

her have that and go on with her life and I'mma go on with mines." Max said right as the phone warned that he two minutes left on the phone call.

Rocky eyes bucked as he looked Azure sitting on the sofa with tears flowing from her eyes. "What pictures bro? What are you talking about? Sis, riding for you. She ain't kicking it with King like that. She still stay in the house with Aunt Nellie. Don't go jumping to conclusions."

"Tell me this, did she come see you when you were in the hospital?" Max asked because he could tell that the pics were taken in a hospital waiting area.

"You know sis was right there with me when I woke up and she came to visit me everyday that I was in there, too. She brought me food and whatever I needed," Rocky said, confidently.

"Well while she was in the room with you, her nigga was waiting on her in the waiting room," Max said right before the phone disconnected.

Azure didn't say anything, she grabbed her purse and she left the trap house without saying goodbye. She had some business to take care of. This call was like the straw that broke the camel's back.

Chapter 16:

King opened the door to his condo with a towel around his waist and on top of his head. He had just gotten out of the shower. He had not been home to his big house in several days and he was running out of clothes.

He could look into her face and tell that she had been crying. He wrapped his massive arms around her and kissed the top of her head. He felt her relax, but he also felt her start back crying. King pulled away from her and lifted her head. He stared into her beautiful blue eyes and knew right then in that instance that he was in love with Azure.

"Tell me what's wrong, so that I can make it right." He planted a kiss on her nose and wrapped his arms back around her.

Azure felt his words in her spirit. She knew he was genuine. All she ever wanted to do was be happy. She wanted the fairy tale that she had always dreamed of. But it was hard to get that when it was a bitch like Fatt Mama waiting in the wings to knock you back every time you took a step forward.

On her way over here, she racked her brain and tried her damndest to come up with a reason why Fatt Mama hated her so much. The only reason she came up with was the fact that she wasn't her. Everything that

Azure had was something that she obtained, but it was also something that was in Fatt Mama's reach, as well. She just would rather take it, than earn it.

"Talk to me, tell me what is wrong. Why are you crying?" King said as he looked down at Azure. She was the most beautiful girl in the world to him.

She didn't want to talk about it. How was she supposed to tell this man who was falling for her that the man she was in love with didn't want her anymore? Azure wrapped her arms around his neck and tugged him forward to signal that she wanted him to kiss her. In her mind, King was kissing her pain away.

His soft lips touched hers and she parted them, sticking her tongue into his mouth, so it could dance against his. King's arms were wrapped around her tightly and she felt so secure, like no one in the world could harm her. A moan escaped from her as shivers went through her. This man was an excellent kisser.

Azure pushed Max far from her mind. 'If you can't love the one you want, love the one you are with.' She pulled her shirt over her head and started back kissing King. He rubbed his hands in her head and up and down her back. The callouses on his hands felt good against her soft skin. She felt him unbutton her bra and she didn't stop him. He took it off and threw it on the floor.

King picked Azure up and placed her on the island. They were almost face-to-face. He grabbed her face and looked her dead in her eyes. "Let me make whatever is wrong right. I want you to be the one I come home to every night. I want to be the one who wins all your fights. I don't want to let you out of my sight." He kissed her lips before he bent down and started to softly nibble on her breasts, alternating from one breast to the other.

All Azure could think about was when her Aunt Nellie told her that she deserved happiness and that happiness was with King. Now she was starting to believe that. It killed her inside to hear Max say those things earlier. It took everything in her to remain silent when he was talking to Rocky. She allowed King to make love to her, hoping that everything on her mind would disappear.

She returned his kisses as her small hands roamed his muscular frame. Her moans grew louder as his warm tongue flicked across her hard nipples while one of his hands teased the other one. He felt the moisture in between her legs start to build up and it was like he read her mind. King lifted Azure off the counter like she was a five-pound bag of sugar and carried her to the bedroom.

He laid her on the bed and unbuttoned her pants and slipped them off of her along with her lace panties. He opened her legs and pulled her to the edge of the bed and buried his head in between her legs.

King lapped at her wetness in the middle before he took her clitoris in his mouth and sucked on it like it was his favorite piece of candy. He alternated between sucking on her magic button and flicking his tongue across it. It was standing up and begging for his attention. Azure's loud moans were driving him wild. He stuck a finger in her middle and she started to grind her hips against his face.

King's head game was definitely top notch. His mouth was so wet, she knew was on the verge of an orgasm and he had just started. As the first one hit her, she closed her eyes tightly and bit down on her lip. She thought that he was going to start back, but instead he was pressing his large rock hard penis into her wetness.

Azure let out a growl when he got as much as he could. She lay on her back and pumped her hips matching him stroke for stroke.

When he bent down and picked her up off the bed she continued to bounce on his huge penis as she kissed him passionately. Azure wrapped her arms around him tightly and held on as he pumped in and out of her vigorously. She could tell that he was about to cum because his grip tightened and he pumped even faster. She felt her orgasm building up too. Their tongues were going wild inside one another's mouth as they kissed while the both of them reached their orgasm. King fell back on the bed, bringing Azure with him, while he was still inside of her.

"We keep this up you are going to end up having my baby," he said as scooted from under her so that she was comfortable.

And just like that the dam broke and she started crying. Azure didn't know what was wrong with her, because she was so emotional lately. "I doubt if I can have any kids. They messed me up pretty bad in there."

He pulled her close to him and held her while smoothing her hair. "Who? Do you want to talk about it?" He was so head over heels with her; he just loved everything about her.

"No, not really. I was pregnant when we got locked up. Someone tried to rape me in the shower when I first got down the road. I fought back and I was beat really bad. I woke up in the infirmary some days later, my womb was empty and I had this scar on my face." Azure inhaled loudly and bit her bottom lip. She was trying to stop the tears from falling, but they just wouldn't.

"I'm so sorry baby. I'm so, so sorry," King said as he smothered her face with kisses and rocked her back and forth in his arms.

Chapter 17:

They had been in the bed talking about everything under the sun. She was feeling a lot better. She remembered her counselor in prison saying sometimes just talking about it was enough. Her stomach growled loudly and King looked at her and laughed.

"I guess I better feed you something, since I have helped you burn all those calories. I only have stuff to make breakfast, is that cool with you? Or do you want to put on something and we go out and eat?" He really didn't want to leave. Behind these walls, his reality didn't exist. As soon as he walked back out the door, he was a business owner and drug king pin whose best friend was just murdered.

"I can eat breakfast all day. Whip up something right quick while I jump in the shower." Azure jumped up off the bed and walked across the room butt naked and headed to the bathroom.

He shook his head, just looking at her made his penis start to get hard again. He grabbed a pair of basketball shorts and slipped them on before going into the kitchen. He took out the ingredients to make a veggie omelet. As he worked on the meal, he thought about what she had said about possibly not being able to have kids.

That wasn't going to stop him. They could always adopt. This woman was going to be his wife.

Azure got out the shower and dried off. She got one of his undershirts out of his underwear drawer and slid it over her head. She grabbed her purse and sat in the middle of the bed in Indian style. She checked her phone. She had missed calls from Rocky, Fatt Mama and Aunt Nellie. She decided to only return her aunt's call.

Azure kept the conversation brief, she told her that she was alright and that she was with King. She also told her that she didn't know if she was coming home at all that night.

She pulled out the manila envelope and ripped it open. She was excited to read the discovery. Her gut was telling her that it was something that she needed to see in it. Azure poured over it reading it faster than she thought. She was flipping from page to page when King came into the bedroom with food on a serving tray. He didn't interrupt her. He just placed the tray with the veggie omelet, whole-wheat toast, and cut up fruit in front of her. He left out and returned to the kitchen to get his plate.

Azure started to eat, but she continued to read. She couldn't believe what she was reading, well she did believe it, she was just in shock. The feds built their case against her; she was not even under their radar. A confidential informant tipped them off. They had been watching Max for years, but they could never build his case because he was very elusive.

"I wonder who in the hell the confidential informant was. I made sure everybody around me was eating damn good. This is fucked up on so many levels. I'm so happy that I ain't get back in the game. It was tempting, though," Azure said with her mouth half full.

"I can find that out. I got people in high places as well as low places." King got off the bed and grabbed his cellphone from off the dresser. He dialed a number and held the phone to his ear as he reached for the stack of papers.

Azure was impressed and she was full. "That omelet was delicious babe."

"Yo D, what's up man? I need a favor. I'm about to give you a case number, I need to find out who the confidential informant is," King said to one of his old college roommates who was now a senior detective in the bureau.

"I'm actually sitting at my desk right now. I need me a woman man. This is my life. I'm either in the field or I'm behind this damn desk." He typed in the number that King gave him.

"Yeah man, I got me a good one for real. You will probably meet her at the funeral." King knew that Azure was the one for him. He felt it in his spirit.

"Okay, I got it. It says that it was a female by the name of Jamesha Jones. Is there anything else you need bro?"

"Jamesha Jones, huh? Did it say that she killed it in or did she actually work hand in hand with you guys?" King asked, curiously.

The minute Azure heard Fatt Mama's real name she turned beet red.

"Oh, she worked hand in hand with the investigators. She came to them with the tip, whoever Azure Knight is, she is in prison because of Jamesha Jones."

"I appreciate it bro, I will see you in a few days," King said ending the call. When he turned around Azure had gotten off the bed and she was putting on her pants.

"Wait a minute, who is Jamesha Jones? Baby where you going? You need to take them pants back off and get in the bed," King said not knowing the seriousness of the matter.

"Jamesha Jones is that bitch Fatt Mama. She has ruined too many lives, too damn many." Azure was pacing back and forth in front of the bed. She was pissed beyond belief. She should have known it.

"That snake bitch. I don't care if I have to take my last dime and put it on her head, I want her dead," Azure spit venomously.

"Be patient, it's a way to do everything. You need a plan. Don't kill her; just make her suffer for the rest of her life," King said. He had never seen Azure this mad before. Her eyes had changed to a blue so dark that they almost looked black. Her entire face was red. She was about to explode. He got up and went up to her and put his arms around her tight.

"Nothing beats the cross, but the double cross. I'm going to help you plan something that she would least expect," King said to Azure. She was stiff and tense as a board.

"She deserves death and nothing less. Fatt Mama is responsible for the robberies and probably a whole slew of other shit if her footsteps were tracked."

King pulled back from Azure and looked at her in face. His bottom lip quivered. "Solo's robbery?"

"Yes! Now do you still want her to suffer for the rest of her life?" Azure asked sarcastically.

"No I'mma kill the bitch with my bare hands," King said, his voice was low and menacing.

THE END….. To Be Continued

Other Books by Sevyn McCray

❖ What Da Lick Read? The Triple Cross

❖ The Real Blockwives of Atlanta

❖ Peach Dollhouse (A sugar babies se ies)

❖ What Da Lick Read 2? Beastmode

❖ The Real Blockwives of Atlanta 2

❖ Side Nigga Chronicles Anthology

www.sevynmccray.com

CONDITION NOTED